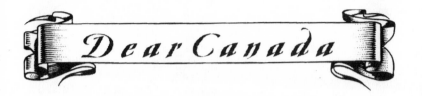

Dear Canada

Not a Nickel to Spare

The Great Depression Diary of Sally Cohen

BY PERRY NODELMAN

Scholastic Canada Ltd.

~~Benjamin Applebaum~~
~~Senior Four, Manning Grove School~~
~~Arithmetic~~
My Diary
By Sally Cohen
Toronto, Ontario, 1932

July 8, 1932

I feel so guilty. I should be upstairs in the kitchen helping Gert do the dishes, not hiding down here in the cellar writing. I shouldn't be writing at all — especially not in this scribbler. But it's too late now. I've already started. I've always wanted to have a diary to write my secrets in, and now's my chance.

Benny gave me this scribbler. He started it just before school ended, but he won't be needing it anymore now, because his pa says he's not going back to school in the fall. Uncle Max called Benny into the kitchen last week after school was over, gave him a paper bag with three hard-boiled eggs and two pieces of bread in it, and told Benny that it was time for him to go out and get a job and try to stop being a useless little @*#!@?!. I can't write down the word that Benny said his pa said. It's too embarrassing. That's why I wrote it like they write bad words in the comics. Even thinking about it makes me blush. I hate to say it, but my Uncle Max is not a very nice person. Maybe that's why Pa doesn't like him and why we hardly ever see him or his family. Except for

Benny, of course. We always see Benny.

Benny is almost fourteen now, so I guess he should have expected it to happen. Uncle Max did the same thing with the bag of eggs and the bread to all of Benny's older brothers and sisters when they were just about the same age. Benny says his pa does it because he's useless and can't hold down a job himself. I wish Benny wouldn't say mean things like that. It's not really Uncle Max's fault. Ma says that ever since he got gassed in the Great War he hasn't been himself.

And anyway, it isn't easy for anyone to keep a job these days. Pa says it's because of the Depression. Pa says it just seems to keep going on and on forever and ever, and there are hardly any jobs and people are always getting laid off and there are hoboes everywhere and nobody has any money. Benny and his brothers and sisters would be starving if his ma wasn't making a few dollars washing floors in some offices on Spadina. Benny's older brothers Sam and Al aren't helping much anymore either, now that they have their own wives to support. I sure hope Benny can find a job soon.

My own pa is working right now, thank goodness, driving the truck just like he does every summer, going out into the country to buy vegetables from farmers and then selling them to the wholesalers at the Fruit Terminal on the Esplanade. But when fall comes and there are no more vegetables growing Pa will be out of work again, too. The only ones in the family bringing in any money will be Sophie, Dora and Gert, and they sure don't make very much cutting and sewing men's pants in Uncle Bertzik's factory. You'd think Uncle Bertzik would pay them more because they're family. But Ma says he can't because it wouldn't be fair to the other girls. So they get peanuts, too, just like the rest.

That's why I feel so guilty about this scribbler. I should have told Ma I had it. Then she wouldn't have to spend a whole 5¢ on another one for me when school starts in September. 5¢ is a lot of money. It's just like I'm taking the food right out of everybody's mouths. How can I be so mean? If Gert knew she'd tell Ma right away. I'm going to have to keep the scribbler hidden down here in the cellar under the orange crates behind the furnace so nobody ever finds out.

Darn! @*#!@?! There's Gert right now, standing in the kitchen and hollering my name so loud that I can hear her right through the floor. She sounds really mad. I am in big trouble. I'd better stop writing and get up there right now.

July 9

I should probably have started by saying who I am. My name is Sally Cohen. I am eleven years old — almost twelve. My birthday is next month, August 22. I live at 29 Leonard Avenue, Toronto, Ontario, Canada with my Ma and Pa, Mr. and Mrs. Moses Cohen, and my five sisters. Sophie is twenty-one, Dora is eighteen, Gert is fifteen, Molly is six, and Hindl just turned four — her birthday was last week. Next year, I will be in Junior Four at Egerton Ryerson Public School. I love to read and I hate to sew. I am small for my age. I am also too skinny, except for my arms, which Gert says are too fat. When I grow up, I am going to be an opera singer.

But back to what happened yesterday when Gert called me. I was right. Boy, was she mad. She gave me a big pinch on my arm, which hurt terribly and left a big blue bruise. But at least she had to do all the dishes by herself, so who cares? I don't. Gert is just a big ugly meanie. Not that I'd ever tell her that, of course, because she'd yell at me and pinch me all over. Why can't she ever be nice to me like Dora always is? Or even just ignore me, the way Sophie usually does? Why did she have to be the one next to me in age?

Just think — if Gert had been born before Dora,

then Sophie would be the one who had to put up with her all the time, and I'd be sharing a bedroom with Dora and doing all my chores with her. That would be heavenly. Dora is so sweet. I'd never try to get out of work if I got to do it with Dora. And even if I did try to get out of it once in a while, Dora would never come all the way down to the library at St. Christopher House, the way Gert did last Thursday night when I got caught up in reading and forgot all about going home and washing the stairs. It was the most embarrassing thing ever. She just burst right in there in front of the librarian and everybody and grabbed me by the collar of my blouse and said, "It's your turn, you *farshtunkener no-goodnik.* Come home right now and do your job." Dora would never do a mean thing like that.

Gert dragged me right out of St. Chris and down the street and all the way home. I couldn't stop crying the whole time I was washing the stairs. My tears were falling down into the bucket. Ma was right behind me the way she always is, cleaning out the cracks with a hairpin, and she didn't even feel sorry for me.

It was all because of *The Five Little Peppers*. It's a wonderful, wonderful book, all about a wonderful family who are really poor but they don't complain and they always love each other and are nice to each other and never pinch each other or drag each other home no matter how poor they are.

Pa says if it's not raining tomorrow we can go for a picnic in the country. I love picnics. I hope there's a beach.

July 11

We drove out into the country yesterday, but we never got to have the picnic. We all went. There was Sophie and her girlfriend Syd Schein, Dora, Gert, me, Molly, Hindl, Ma and Pa, my Auntie Bella, my Auntie Fanny, and my cousins Yenta, Humty, Millie, Shaindl and Goldie. They are all sisters and all girls, of course, just like our family. Poor Pa — he's always surrounded by girls and women. He says it's like being in a harem. But of course he's still the boss.

Pa drove and Ma sat beside him, and the rest of us sat in the back on some boards we put on top of orange crates. It was a beautiful sunny day. It was ever so heavenly to drive down the highway like that with the wind in my hair. We sang all the songs we knew, Yiddish ones and school songs and even songs from the radio like "Tea for Two" and "I Found a Million Dollar Baby in the Five and Ten Cent Store." I sang as high as I possibly could, just like the opera singers do, and imagined what it would be like to have curly blond hair and thin arms and sing live on the stage of the Metropolitan Opera House in New York City while millions listened on their radios all across America. Just like me and Sophie did every Saturday afternoon all last winter. We had to listen to the station in Buffalo and the sound was awful, but it was worth it.

After driving for a long time and singing until we were all hoarse, we came to a sign for a private beach, and Pa turned the truck off the highway onto the dirt road. But then he suddenly stopped. I couldn't figure out why until Shaindl pointed to a big sign that was standing beside the road. It said *NO JEWS OR DOGS ALLOWED.*

Why not? It didn't make any sense to me. I mean, I can see why somebody wouldn't want a dog on their beach. Dogs bark all the time in a very scary way. They bite innocent strangers for no reason, and they go to the toilet wherever they feel like it, which is disgusting. What if someone came out of the water and accidentally stepped in it? It would be awful.

But what's wrong with having Jews on a beach? Jews don't bark or bite and they always use the toilet room — even Hindl. The whole thing was just plain silly. As Pa began to back the truck out onto the highway again, I asked Sophie about it. Sophie always knows everything. But she just sat there looking very upset and told me to *sha shtil*. I didn't want to shut up. I was about to ask her again when there was a very loud bang. Very, very loud. The whole truck shook and then came to a stop.

Pa had backed the truck out onto the highway and right into a big fancy limousine. The kind millionaires and movie stars drive.

It was a complete mess. Everybody fell off the boards they were sitting on. Gert, Humty and Dora, who were sitting closest to the front, bumped the backs of their heads on the back window of the truck, and the rest of us just fell all over each other. The little ones were all screaming at the top of their lungs. To tell the truth, I was, too, and so was Gert. It was so scary. Ma rushed out of one side of the truck and Pa out of the other, and they were both reaching up into the truck and trying to get hold of us and shouting, *"Gevalt, gevalt!* Are you hurt? Is everybody all right? *Oy gevalt!"*

It took a while for everyone to calm down and stop screaming. When we did, it turned out that nobody was hurt, not even a little bruise, *kayn ayn-horeh*. It's a good thing Pa was going so slow.

But then the man from the limousine came over and started shouting at Pa. He was a big *goyishe* man with a bald head, a big stomach and very red face. He was very, very angry. Every second word was

@*#!@?! But of course Pa was so upset he couldn't understand all of what the man was shouting about and just kept shouting back in Yiddish. Pa used a lot of words I've never heard before, but I think they also meant @*#!@?! — only in Yiddish.

Finally, the man calmed down enough for Sophie to tell him that Pa didn't understand much English. So then the man started shouting at her instead. He was furious that his expensive new car was damaged. I don't know why he was so upset. It was just a tiny little dent in the door, and the back of Pa's truck had a dent, too. And anyway, it was the man's fault, really, because he should have been watching where he was going. Pa was going so slow, he really and truly was. He's a very, very careful driver. People are always honking their horns at him to get him to drive faster. Anyway, the man finally calmed down enough to write Pa's name and address and licence number. Then he said we shouldn't think this was over, not by a long shot, and we'd be hearing more about it from the police. He slammed shut the door of his limousine and drove off.

Well, after that, of course, nobody felt like having a picnic. We just turned around and drove right back into the city and home again. We didn't sing a single song. We ate our sandwiches in the dining room.

It was the stupid sign that caused all the trouble.

I still don't understand it, and nobody will explain it to me. Not even Sophie, and she loves to explain things. Maybe Benny will know.

July 12

I talked to Benny about the sign. I guess he and I are sort of best friends — even if he is annoying. And a boy, which is really annoying.

Trust me to end up with a boy for a best friend. It certainly isn't very ladylike. I bet Queen Mary or Lady Flora Eaton don't talk about important things with any boys — especially not annoying ones like Benny. But at least Benny listens to me, not like Gert or Sophie. And Dora listens but she just agrees with everything I say, which is nice, I guess, but not very interesting.

There are the girls at school of course — and there's Rivka Goldstein in my class who lives across the street and plays with me sometimes. But all she ever wants to do is play with her dolls and talk about movie stars and the latest fashions. It's so, so boring. At least Benny doesn't ever want to play with dolls.

Benny got really angry when I told him about the sign. He said the *goyim* are all *anti-semits*. They're not Jewish and so they hate Jews. They hate anyone who is the least bit different from themselves, but they especially hate Jews. Some of them even think that when someone has Jewish blood in them it means that that person isn't as good as they are. Back in the old country, Benny says, there are whole political parties who want to get into power so that they can stop Jews from speaking Jewish or even having businesses. They're in Germany, and they're called Nazis. Benny's Pa told him all about it. Some of them even want to kick all the Jews out of their country. And some of the *goyim* here in Canada agree with them.

Benny says that's probably why that sign was there at the beach. Benny says that if we Jews don't wake up a little and start defending ourselves, we might all be in big, big trouble.

I think Benny's a fool, and I told him so, too. It's just silly. Canada is a free country, isn't it? And we may be Jewish, but we're Canadians, too. British citizens. Even Ma and Pa are, because even though they were born in the old country they became citizens last year, and Pa has the papers to prove it. And if we're British citizens, then they can't stop us from going to the beach, can they? Of course not. It makes no sense.

Benny said I was just a big dumb baby who didn't know anything about anything — *gornisht*, nothing. He laughed at me. Sometimes he makes me so mad. It would serve him right if I put up a big sign on the front door that said *NO DOGS OR BENNYS ALLOWED.*

July 22

It's been such a long time since I wrote anything in this scribbler. I didn't have anything to write. It's a funny thing about summer. You spend all winter just waiting for school to be over, and then when it is, it's so boring. I haven't done anything for days and days but read *The Five Little Peppers*. I actually finished it last week and I took it back to St. Chris and looked for a new book, but nothing seemed to be anywhere near as interesting, so I just kept *The Five Little Peppers* and started to read it again. It's still wonderful, but I wish I didn't already know what's going to happen before it happens. Just like my whole boring life.

I mean really, it's truly and completely awful. I do the same things at the same time day after day after day. Gosh, I even eat the same food. I wake up every morning at ten to seven when I hear Pa getting ready for work, and I always have the same cup of cocoa and the same slice of bread for breakfast. Sometimes I get a bagel. Lucky me. At least now Pa is working, so we can buy the good Fry's cocoa instead of that horrible cheap kind from Eaton's that hardly even tastes like chocolate. But then every day for lunch we have the same cottage cheese with sour cream on top and the same salad with lettuce and tomatoes that Pa gets from the market. And every Monday I help Ma do the washing and we have the same old mashed potatoes and hard-boiled eggs for supper. And every Tuesday I look after Molly and Hindl while Ma does the ironing and we have cabbage for supper and it stinks up the house. And on Wednesday I look after Molly and Hindl while Ma sews and mends and on Thursday Ma goes over to the market and does the shopping and we wash the floors and clean the house. And on Friday Ma makes *gefilte* fish and boiled chicken and *kugel* and we have compote for dessert, and she lights the candles and we have Shabbes. And on Saturday Ma and Pa go to *shul*, and on Sunday Pa stays home and we have herrings and potatoes for breakfast. And then it's Monday again.

Today it's Friday. Yesterday we washed the floors and Ma went shopping, and today she made *gefilte* fish and chicken and *kugel* and compote. It'll soon be sundown and I'll have to stop writing because Pa says writing is work even if you're just doing it for fun, so I won't be able to write anything more until Shabbes is over at sundown tomorrow.

Today's compote is stewed prunes. I hate stewed prunes.

I can't wait for school to start again.

July 26

I went out to get the milk this morning and guess who was on the veranda? Benny, that's who. He was sleeping on the stinky old couch we have out there that's always getting rained on. I refuse to even sit on it, but Benny was so sound asleep, he didn't even hear the milkman come up on the veranda. I wish I could sleep like that, and then I wouldn't have to listen to Gert snore and gurgle all night. It's disgusting. I think she does it on purpose just to keep me awake.

Anyway, I knew Pa would be mad if he found Benny out there, so I shook Benny until he woke up and asked him what he was doing there. He said he came over in the middle of the night but the house was dark and he didn't want to wake anybody up so he just stayed outside. He came because his pa got really mad at him and hit him again. His cheek was still red from it. Uncle Max got mad because

Later

I had to stop writing and hide my scribbler real fast because I heard the cellar door open. It was just

Molly. She wanted someone to tie her shoes and no one else would do it. She's old enough to do it by herself by now. Poor Molly. She's so quiet and the house is so full of noisy people that no one ever notices her. I think she just wants some attention.

Anyway, where was I? Oh yes, Uncle Max got mad because he found out that Benny made some money selling newspapers on the street, and he told Benny to give it to him. But Benny refused, because when his pa gets money he usually just spends it on himself — on alcohol, Benny says, except Benny calls it booze. Benny wants to give the money to his ma so she can buy food for the family, like his older brothers and sisters do when they have any money to spare. Benny has a good heart, even if he is a pest.

But I guess Uncle Max doesn't know about that, because he asked Benny if he thought he was better than the rest of the family. He asked Benny if he thought he was a prince or something, keeping all his money to himself like that, and he bowed to him and called him Prince Benjamin the First. Imagine! Anyway, that's when Benny called Uncle Max a bad name with @*#!*?! in it, and that's when Uncle Max hit Benny. Maybe Pa is right about Uncle Max.

After that, Benny got out of there as fast as he could and wandered around in the dark for a long time because he didn't want to go back home and get hit again, and then finally he came here and slept on the veranda. I felt so sorry for him I gave him my breakfast bagel, and now I am so hungry I could die and it's still two hours to lunch. Benny is such a nuisance. I wish I didn't like him so much.

August 1

I am in Wasaga Beach! I'm going to be here for an entire week!

It's all because of Ma. Sophie's friend Syd Schein invited Sophie to come with her to the beach. Syd was going to go with another friend who couldn't come at the last minute because her *zayde* died and she had to sit *shiva,* but she'd already paid for the hotel and they wouldn't give her her money back and she said she was willing to let Sophie go in her place if Sophie paid half the price. Sophie told Syd she couldn't even afford that, but Syd's friend was desperate and said Sophie could have the room anyway and just give her whatever she could afford. Sophie wouldn't tell me what she agreed to pay, but I know it was a lot. And then there's the bus fare, too. It sounded to me like we just can't afford it, but Sophie told Ma it was a real bargain and she promised to give Ma all her wages all winter and not keep anything for herself if Ma would let her go. I was really surprised, because Sophie is usually so sensible and she knows we don't have any money to spare even if Pa is working now. What will we do when winter comes?

Sophie begged and pleaded until Ma finally agreed to let her go. But Ma said Sophie couldn't go unless she took me with her. Ma figured there'd be a children's fare on the bus and the hotel wouldn't charge Sophie for having a child in the same room, and she was right, but we do have to pay for a cot for me — 25¢ a night.

Ma is the best mother ever. It'll be awful spending my whole time with Sophie and being told to stand up straight fifteen times an hour and getting lectures about how I need to learn good manners and long division so I can be a credit to the family. And the cot is very lumpy. But it's the beach! It'll be worth it.

I don't know how Ma will find the money, though. I hope she doesn't take in piecework again like she did last winter, because all that sewing gives her terrible headaches. Maybe she'll get the money from Uncle Bertzik. And what will Pa say when he finds out?

Just before we left the house, I remembered about the scribbler being under the orange crates, and I rushed down and got it and stuck it in my bag. If anyone found it while I wasn't there and read what I said about them, I would just die.

The bus trip seemed to go on forever, but the beach is divine. People drive right onto the sand and park their cars near the water. It's ever so sophisticated.

We're staying at a resort called the Wasaga Inn. It's very big and very nice, I guess. But as far as I can tell, none of the other people staying here are Jewish. They sure don't act Jewish — more like glamorous people in movies.

Also, Sophie told me not to tell anyone here that we're Jewish. I don't see why not. I mean, they don't have a sign out about Jews and dogs, do they? So what's she worried about anyway? Sophie says she isn't worried, but we live in Canada, and we should act like Canadians. I don't see how not saying you're Jewish makes you a Canadian. But Sophie thinks it does. She even refuses to speak Yiddish anymore, even at home. It makes Pa furious. I wish Sophie and Pa got along better.

For breakfast this morning, Sophie and Syd ordered bacon and eggs. Bacon is from pigs! It's *trayf*! I guess I must have looked shocked that they were having food Jews aren't allowed to eat, because they started to tease me. They said that only old-fashioned fools keep kosher anymore because it's just a silly old superstition, and it's the twentieth century now, and there's nothing wrong with eating bacon. They said it was delicious even if it did come from a pig and I should have some, too.

I didn't want them to think I was a fraidy-cat, so I did order some. But when it came, just looking at it made me gag. Sophie and Syd laughed at me, and Sophie said, "Too bad, more for me," and ate it all herself. Sophie is so smart and so sophisticated, and with the new haircut she got last month, she looks just like Joan Crawford. Joan Crawford is definitely not my favourite movie star, but she is a movie star. Maybe tomorrow I'll try to eat bacon again.

August 2

We spent all day sitting on the beach. Syd got a terrible sunburn, but Sophie is so dark she just got a good tan and now she looks even more like Joan Crawford. Nothing happened to me, of course, because I kept a towel around my shoulders all day so nobody would laugh at how skinny I am. I did go in the water once, but it was ever so cold and I came right out again. I just sat there and ate the cherries that Sophie brought with her from Toronto and pretended to read my book while Syd and Sophie talked about movie stars and politics and the opera and what to eat to keep slim and all sorts of other things. Syd and Sophie think they know everything.

Now they've gone to the Dardanella. It's a dance hall, and children aren't allowed, so they told me I had to stay here in the room all by myself. They get to go out and dance all the new steps they've been learning with each other while I have nothing to do but sit here and write and eat more cherries, but I bet it's better than being in a dance hall and getting stared at by strange men. What would Pa say if he knew? You won't catch me going to awful places like that when I'm a grown-up.

August 3

Sophie is furious with me. Is it my fault I got sick?

Sophie says it is. She says it was because of all the cherries I ate, but what does she know? Maybe it was and maybe it wasn't. Besides, she's the one who brought the cherries, not me. If you ask me, it's her fault.

Anyway, my stomach was churning and I lay on the bed and felt awful for hours and hours, except for all the time I was in the toilet room, which was a lot. When Sophie and Syd came back from the dance I told Sophie I was going to die and I apologized for being so mean to her and getting her into trouble with Ma and Pa for killing me with cherries at the beach. But she just gave me a dirty look and asked how many cherries I'd eaten. When I told her, she said, "I might have known," and made me go to bed. And she hasn't said a word to me since. She just left me here in the room feeling sick all day while she went to sit on the beach with Syd. She didn't even say she was happy a while ago when I told her I was feeling a little better. She just ignores me and acts like I'm not here at all.

I still think it's *her* fault.

August 5

The sun is still up so it isn't Shabbes yet. But it will be soon — and Sophie has gone out to the Dardanella again. She's going to dance on Shabbes, in public! And she didn't even think about lighting the candles.

It's the first Shabbes that I've ever been away from home, and I'm going to miss Ma saying the prayers. I could try to say them myself, I guess, but I don't *have* any candles. And anyway the cot is too lumpy and I feel worse than I have all day. I want to go home.

I feel much better. But I am never eating cherries ever again.

While we were sitting on the beach this afternoon, a man came up to us and said hello to Sophie. I thought she'd just tell him to go away because she's a nice Jewish girl, not the kind of shameless hussy in movies who wears too much makeup and talks to strangers on the beach. But she didn't. Even without any makeup on, she said hello right back. She even said his name, which is Steven. What an ugly name.

It seems that Sophie met this Steven person at the Dardanella the other night. And she even danced with him! And she did it again last night! Imagine, my own sister Sophie, dancing with a man! And she's not even related to him! If Pa only knew.

Anyway, Steven sat down with us right on our blanket and he and Sophie talked about all the books they'd read. Steven adores *The Good Earth* by Pearl S. Buck, just like Sophie. I started to read it while Sophie had the copy she borrowed from Syd, but Sophie caught me and told me I was too young for it. I don't care — it seemed to be all about people starving in China, and nobody was happy, not for a moment. Not like the Five Little Peppers in their cozy Little Brown House. Steven seems kind of nice,

I guess, for a man — if you forget about all the freckles and the bright red hair.

August 7

It's hard to believe it's been a whole week already. We'll be taking the bus back to Toronto tomorrow, and I didn't do anything but sit on the beach and read. I've read *The Five Little Peppers* three times now. I bet I could almost recite it word for word with the book closed. I'll be so happy to get to the library and find another book.

I've also been going to stores and things with Syd. Poor Syd. She has to take me because Sophie has been spending all her time with Steven. I guess Sophie and Steven have a lot in common, even if she looks like Joan Crawford and he looks sort of like what Blackie in the Ella Cinders comic strip would look like if he were a grown-up and had red hair instead of black.

He talks about boring politics and philosophers and things, just like Sophie. He even likes listening to the opera, and his favourite one on the radio last year was *Romeo and Juliet,* just like me. It was all in French or Italian or something, but I could tell it was sad and lovely even if I didn't understand the words.

But there's one thing that Sophie and Steven don't have in common. Steven isn't Jewish.

Really! He isn't! Syd says she thinks Sophie is crazy for even letting him talk to her, and so do I. In my opinion, you should stick to your own kind, like Pa says. I mean, gosh, what if Steven comes from a family that put up one of those *No Jews or Dogs* signs? I don't know what Sophie is thinking of. It probably comes from eating all that bacon.

August 8

It was nice to go away, but it's nice to be back home, too. I didn't realize how much I missed the little ones until Molly and Hindl saw Sophie and me coming down the street and came rushing out the door and gave me a big hug. Molly even coloured a special picture for me of me on the beach with a big sun shining on me. Poor Molly — she must have been so lonely while I was gone. Ma said Molly and Hindl were waiting by the window in the parlour all morning. Usually she doesn't even let them in there unless it's Shabbes.

Ma gave me a big hug, too, and so did Dora, and even Gert said she was glad to see me. She was, too — but it was mostly because Pa made her go to the Fruit Terminal with him to do the accounts because

I wasn't there to do them like I usually do. Gert hates arithmetic, and she's terrible at it. Now that I'm back, I'm going to have to fix all her mistakes. Pa says it'll probably take me all day because she made so many. He was just joking, but Gert stopped smiling at me and went back to looking the mean way she usually does. Why do I have to be the smart one?

Sophie didn't tell Ma about the cherries. Maybe she's not so bad after all.

August 9

I went to the library to take *The Five Little Peppers* back, and Miss Pugh, the lady who works in that room, told me the most exciting thing. She says there are more books about the Five Little Peppers! Lots and lots of them! They don't have them in the library at St. Chris, but I'm going to ask Ma if I can go to Boys and Girls House behind the big library on College Street and see if they have them there. Maybe tomorrow or later this week.

I had to go with Pa to the Fruit Terminal to work on the accounts (which were a real mess, thanks to Gert). While I was there I spotted the same bunch of little kids I saw there a few times before I went to the beach. They are much younger than me, and their clothes are filthy and full of holes and they have no shoes. They were going through the garbage just like they did the last time I saw them, picking out the wilted lettuce and squashed tomatoes and then running off with it. Pa says they come all the time, and the men at the Terminal just pretend not to notice them because it might be just about the only food they and their families get. The Depression is such an awful thing, and we are so, so lucky. At least we have food and shoes.

August 11

I got two more Five Little Peppers books, *The Five Little Peppers Midway* and *The Five Little Peppers Grown Up*. I can't wait to read them.

And I have a secret! A terrible secret. While I was walking down College Street on my way home from the big library, I saw Sophie getting off the streetcar from downtown, so I ran up to meet her and walk home with her. She didn't look very happy to see me. She kept looking over her shoulder at the streetcar. I guess she shouldn't have done that, because it made me look at the streetcar, too, and you'll never guess what I saw. There was a man with bright red hair and lots of freckles! He was leaning his head against the window and giving Sophie a wave as the streetcar pulled away!

I'm not really, truly sure, but I think it was that man Steven from Wasaga Beach. I asked Sophie if it was and she said, no, I must be *meshugge*, of course not. But I bet it was him. I bet Sophie was on a date with him. Sophie on a date, that's bad enough! But with a *shaygetz! Oy.* Should I tell Ma and Pa? Sophie didn't tell about the cherries. I don't know what to do.

August 16

I was thinking about that man on the streetcar all weekend, and I almost decided to tell Ma and Pa. But then yesterday a letter came for Pa and it was from the police! It said the man whose car we ran into last month filed a complaint and we'll be getting a letter next month about going to court. Imagine, my own father, in court, like a criminal! Pa is always so good. He never did anything bad to anybody in his entire life. Life is so unfair.

Pa was so upset, and Ma, too. She cried and cried, and he shouted a lot about how nobody respects him like they did in the old country and then he went out to the backyard and smoked about ten cigarettes in a row and wouldn't talk to anybody.

Anyway, after we got the letter I decided not to say anything about the man on the streetcar. Ma and Pa already have so much to worry about. It probably wasn't Steven anyway. That man was probably waving at somebody else, not Sophie. Sophie is too smart to do something like that.

Benny heard about Pa's letter from his ma, who heard it from someone on her street who knew the mother of a friend of Gert's who heard it from Gert, and he came over to tell me it showed he was right about the Nazis. He says he read in one of the *Toronto Daily Stars* he was selling last week that the Nazis have fourteen million followers in Germany and each and every one of them hates Jews. Their leader is a man called Hitler, and he might even become the chancellor soon. Benny says that's like being the prime minister here in Canada. Hitler sounds like Hettler, which is the name of the people who have the little store near the corner on Nassau. But I guess this Hitler can't be Jewish like they are, because Benny said Hitler is a terrible *anti-semit* and he bets the man in the limousine is one, too, and so are the police and so are all the judges right here in Toronto and everyone knows it.

I told him he was wrong. I sure hope he is.

August 21

This morning, Ma let me climb up into the pear tree in the backyard and pick three — one for me, one for Molly and one for Hindl. I think they taste good even if they are a little bit sour. But I guess Molly doesn't agree, because I took her and Hindl around the corner to the park, and while I was busy pushing Hindl on the swing, Molly went off by herself across the park and gave her pear to a man who was lying on a bench under some old newspapers. It really surprised me — she's usually so shy. When I noticed, I had to grab Hindl off the swing and rush over there and drag Molly away, and both girls ended up crying at the top of their voices and so did I. It was very embarrassing.

On the way home I told Molly she should know better than to talk to strangers — especially ones as filthy and stinky as that man was. But Molly said she didn't like the pear and anyway, the man looked like he needed it more than she did. That was really sweet of her, but I didn't let her know I thought so. There are so many hoboes around nowadays, and she has to learn to be more careful.

Although I have to admit that the man on the bench didn't look very dangerous. He wasn't really a man. He couldn't be much older than Benny. And he was even skinnier than Benny and he looked very weak and sick and he was totally covered in soot. He must be one of those unemployed people Sophie told me about who sneak onto trains to go to a different town and try to find a job. Sophie says there are thousands of them now, riding the rails all over Canada, and nobody will give a job to strangers like them, so they just have to beg for handouts and then get back on the train and try again somewhere else, and they can't go back home because the people there say they don't belong there anymore either. Sophie says it serves them right, but it must be awful, being on your own like that. I guess I'm glad Molly gave that boy her pear, even if she shouldn't have done it.

The Five Little Peppers Midway is pretty good. I thought it would be about the Peppers going to the Exhibition and riding rides on the midway, but it isn't, thank goodness. I don't like the midway. It's about the Peppers growing up and getting happier and richer.

August 22

It was my birthday today. I am twelve now. Ma gave me a big kiss when I came down for breakfast, and then baked a special cake for me! After supper, we all sang "Happy Birthday," and Gert gave me a pinch to grow an inch. If Gert pinching me really made me grow I'd be about twenty feet tall by now. Still, I wish it would work. I hate being short.

August 23

Benny came over to tell me he has a new job, but he wouldn't say what it is, just that it's at the Ex, on the midway. He says if I want to know what it is I have to come and see for myself. I said I couldn't because I didn't have the money to get in, but he says he'll give it to me himself because he's going to be making a fortune.

I wonder what he'll be doing. I guess I'll have to go and find out, even if I do hate the midway. It's always so noisy and crowded there, and the people in the little booths where you throw baseballs or darts or other things to win prizes call you "girlie" when you walk by and make fun of you when you pretend you can't hear them. But Benny made his job sound so mysterious and exciting. If I don't find out what it is, I'll just die. I hope it isn't against the law.

The best thing is, he won't be selling papers anymore, and I won't have to hear him go on and on all the time about how awful the Nazis are and how they're assaulting Jews on the streets in Germany now. Ma says no news is good news, and I agree.

August 30

I didn't have to get money from Benny, because yesterday Dora took me with her to the Ex. I don't know where she got the money, because she always gives everything she earns to Ma. But Ma didn't know we were going and Dora didn't say where we'd been when we got back. So I've decided I won't ask. Sometimes it's better not to know.

Dora says she really loves the Ex, and so do I, except for the midway. It goes on forever. People say it's the biggest annual exhibition in the entire world — and it's right here in Toronto! It's too noisy, but I have to admit it's exciting. There are people everywhere selling popcorn and fried potatoes and roasted peanuts and other food that smells so good, even if Pa says it's probably all *trayf* and Jewish people like us can't eat it. It's a good thing it's too expensive for us to afford, or else I'd probably want to buy some and that would be bad.

But there are lots and lots of things to see, champion horses and cats and other animals on display and this year there's a whole building full of things from China called the Forbidden City. I don't know why it's called forbidden, because it was just boring old pots and paintings and things. If Sophie saw it, she'd love it — or at least she'd say she loved it, but she'd probably really find it just as dull as Dora and I did. Sophie is always pretending to be so, so sophisticated, talking about art and eating bacon and saying everyone else has such bad taste. But last week I caught her looking at a movie magazine Gert borrowed from one of the girls at work, and she was so interested in reading the gossip that she didn't even see me.

After a few minutes in the Forbidden City, we decided the Pure Food Building would be more interesting. We each got a whole shopping bag full of free samples, Shredded Wheat and gum and pamphlets about gelatin and baking powder and so many other things. We'll probably throw most of the pamphlets out right away without even looking at them, but they were free, so we took them.

After that, we went to a fashion show in the Fashion Building. The clothes were simply divine. I especially liked a white, sleeveless slack suit with a red and blue stripe across the top. It had a V-neck and the pants flared out at the bottom like sailor pants, and there was even a cute little matching hat. It was adorable. Of course, I could never wear a suit like that myself. It would just show off my arms, and Gert would be sure to say something mean. Maybe I could wear it with a sweater on top.

I've written so much today that my pencil is getting dull. I need to sharpen it.

That's better. After the fashion show, I made Dora take me to the midway to find Benny. It was just as awful as it always is. A horrible man shouted that he was going to guess my weight, but luckily he didn't. I'd have died if he said it out loud right in front of the crowd. But they all laughed when I turned bright red, and that was almost as bad.

To get to where Benny and his sisters were, we had to go by the Ubangi Belles. They were dark people from Africa and they had big stretched-out lower lips you could put a whole saucer inside of and they were wearing almost nothing and dancing like crazy. They were pretending to be happy, but their eyes looked so sad it almost made me cry. The man there wanted people to pay to go inside and see them dance more. Why would anybody want to do that? People are *meshugge*.

When we got to the place where Benny worked, his sisters were standing in front of a little tank filled with water. There were wearing nothing but their bathing suits! Right there on the midway! They should be ashamed of themselves. It's so embarrassing, knowing that those girls showing themselves off like that are your cousins, your own flesh and blood, even though I don't know them very well because they're so much older than me, and anyway, Benny is the only one in their family who comes around to our place very often and we hardly ever see them.

At least Rosie and Ruthie look good in a bathing suit. They're both so pretty, like movie stars. I hope

I look like them when I grow up. But even if I did, I wouldn't show off in a bathing suit in public in broad daylight.

When we got there, Rosie and Ruthie were pointing to Benny, who was standing on a ladder behind the pool. He was wearing a bathing suit too, and all his ribs were sticking out. But at least he looked cleaner than he usually does. Rosie and Ruthie were shouting at the crowd, asking people to throw coins into the pool and if they did, then Benny would dive into the pool and try to get them.

Benny doesn't know how to dive and he can't swim. He must have nearly drowned every time he jumped into the tank. The time Dora and I saw him he came up sputtering and coughing and could hardly make it to the edge of the tank. What was he thinking of? What were Rosie and Ruthie thinking of to let him do it?

Well, at least he's not doing it anymore. After the show was over, Dora and I went up to the stage to say hello to Benny and Rosie and Ruthie, and when we got there they were all shouting at each other and looking really upset. It was because Ruthie and Rosie wanted Benny to give them some of the money he got from the pool. They said he didn't deserve it all because the audience just threw the coins into the water because they liked the way they looked in their bathing suits. Benny got so mad he threw all the coins back into the pool and told them to go get them themselves. Then he stomped behind the curtain to get his clothes and never came back. I guess he's back to selling newspapers again. It serves him right, but I can't help feeling sorry for him.

September 1

There was an eclipse of the sun yesterday.

When I heard about it on the radio I got really excited. It sounded so mysterious and so thrilling. But yesterday afternoon when the eclipse started I was afraid to look. Sophie said you had to have smoked glasses because looking right at the eclipse without them could make you blind, and of course we didn't have any smoked glasses and I don't want to be blind. So I sort of squinched my eyes and looked close to the sun but not right at it. It got dark for a bit, kind of, but I didn't really see anything special.

Well, at least I know it happened.

September 6

School started today. Finally.

Now that I'm in Junior Four, I'll be using the 14¢ reader. A whole book of new stories and poems — I can hardly wait! I went over to Auntie Bella's and got the reader from my cousin Millie yesterday. Millie used it last year, and she got it from Gert, who scribbled her name all over it, of course, right across some perfectly divine poems. Sometimes Gert makes me want to scream.

At least I have a reader. If I keep going to school next year like Ma and Pa and Sophie say they want me to, the reader will cost 16¢, and no one else in the family has gone that far in school yet, so we'll have to buy a new one. I do like school, but the books and the scribblers are so expensive and anyway I want to go out and earn money and help the family like Sophie and Dora and even Gert do. Why do I have to be the smart one?

Rivka from across the street is in my class again, and my teacher is Miss Douglas. I think she's going to be nice. She has lovely brown hair and today she wore a lovely navy blue dress with a pleated skirt and cute little capped sleeves in lace and she said that Sally was a perfectly lovely name. So who cares if she's not Jewish?

Benny does, that's who. Benny says she's not Jewish because there aren't any Jewish teachers at all. Benny says Jews aren't allowed to be teachers or doctors or lawyers or even work on the streetcars or get jobs as sales clerks at Eaton's, and since the

Depression started Jews can't even get the jobs they used to get because the *goyim* keep them all for themselves. Benny says it's almost as bad here as it is in Germany, and if you ask him, that's pretty bad.

I wish Benny would stop selling newspapers and go work in Uncle Bertzik's factory. Then he wouldn't be reading about all the horrible things happening in Germany and he could stop worrying about them and trying to get me to worry about them, too. Pa is so upset about going to court, and Sophie says she's going out with Syd all the time, but I saw Syd in the market yesterday without Sophie when Sophie said she was going to see her. I have enough to worry about already.

September 7

We had Domestic Science for the first time today. The teacher handed out squares of flannelette and said we have to make underpants out of them. Underpants! Really! It was all right today, because it was just a piece of flannelette. But as soon as we cut them out, they'll start to look like underpants, and we'll be working on them right in front of each other. Even just thinking about it makes me blush.

September 8

I got every answer right in my arithmetic test yesterday. So did one of the *goyishe* girls, Myrtle MacDonald. But Myrtle had two errors in spelling and I just had one. Myrtle seems kind of nice, even if she isn't Jewish.

September 15

Sophie and Pa are furious with each other, and it's all my fault. I guess maybe I should have told Ma about that man on the streetcar. How was I supposed to know what would happen?

It all started on Monday night when these strangers rang the doorbell. It was a *goyishe* man and lady. They said they were Mr. and Mrs. Hayward, and they wanted to see Ma and Pa. Ma and Pa took them into the parlour and closed the door, and Gert and I tried to hear what they were saying but we couldn't, except for once when Pa shouted but we couldn't make out what he said. When they came out, Mr. and Mrs. Hayward looked angry and Pa's face was bright red and Ma was trying not to cry but she was crying anyway. I didn't know why until Sophie came home later.

Mr. and Mrs. Hayward are Steven's parents! I should have guessed, because Mr. Hayward had freckles and red hair just like his.

And you'll never guess why they came! They came because Steven told them he was engaged to Sophie! To be married!

Steven's parents told Ma and Pa they didn't approve of him marrying a Jewish girl, especially since Mr. Hayward is a minister in the United Church. Imagine, a church minister in our house! But Mr. Hayward said Steven was a grown man with a mind of his own and they had to accept it. They said that Steven had brought Sophie over to meet them and they thought she was a lovely girl even if she was Jewish, and they thought it was time to meet her family. That's why they came.

Imagine, Sophie, who's always telling the rest of us how to behave properly, sneaking around like that behind everyone's backs. And getting engaged to a *goy*! A *goy* with a church minister for a father! And none of us knew a single thing about it.

Except me — and I didn't tell, because of the cherries. I just feel so awful.

As soon as Sophie walked in the door, Pa started yelling at her and saying she was a sneak and a liar and a monster, and he made her tell him what was going on. Sophie began to cry like crazy and she told him it was all true and she wasn't ashamed of anything. She knew he wouldn't approve and that's why she didn't say anything, but she was going to marry Steven whether Pa liked it or not, because she loved him and he loved her and they were meant to be together and it was a free country and it was the twentieth century now, not the Dark Ages.

It was almost like a movie. If it was Joan Crawford talking about Clark Gable or John Barrymore and not just my own sister Sophie talking about Steven, it would have been ever so romantic.

But it made Pa even madder. It was awful. I've never seen him like that, not ever. He's usually so quiet. He said Sophie was trying to destroy the family and the whole Jewish race and he wasn't going to stand for it. He told her he'd kill himself if she married that *goy*, and he even grabbed the big sharp knife that Ma uses for cutting up chickens and started waving it around while he shouted. Ma was screaming at him to calm down and Sophie was still crying like crazy and telling him to stop, and so were all the rest of us, even Hindl. Finally, Sophie said she'd break off the engagement if Pa would just put the knife down, and he stopped shouting and stared at her, and she stared back and said nothing, just shook, and finally, he dropped the knife and she started crying again and ran off to her room. Pa started shouting at her again, even after she was gone, and then he stomped out, too. I think he went to the *shul* to pray. Ma went up to Sophie with a cup of tea, but Sophie wouldn't take it. She said her heart was broken and she just wanted to die.

She hasn't died yet. But she and Pa haven't said a word to each other since.

I wrote so much today that I had to sharpen my pencil twice. Lucky I got some free ones at the Ex.

September 16

Sophie spent all day in her room. A friend of Steven's came to the door with a note from him for Sophie. She wouldn't even come down to get it, but Ma took it up to her and after a while she brought a note back from Sophie for Steven. Then Ma went back upstairs, and afterwards we could hear them both crying.

September 19

Sophie met Steven yesterday to tell him the engagement was off and she could never see him again. Ma told us about it so we would understand if Sophie was upset when she came home. She was, too. She had tear stains on her face and she looked just awful. I wish I could have been there. It must have been so sad and so beautiful, even if it was just in Altman's delicatessen on College Street surrounded by people eating corned-beef sandwiches and pickles and Sophie made Syd go with her. But I'm glad Sophie came to her senses. Steven has so many freckles.

And Pa is right. We should stick to our own kind. Last week I was thinking I might actually talk to that girl in my class, Myrtle MacDonald, even if it made Rivka and some of the other Jewish girls angry, because Miss Douglas said Myrtle liked writing stories, too, just like me, and nobody else I know likes doing the things I do. But now I'm not going to, because no matter how much she likes writing, Myrtle is still not Jewish.

September 22

The letter finally came today to tell Pa when he has to go to court. It's next month, on October 12.

Poor Pa. He started to shake when I read the letter out to him. Sophie felt so bad for him that she actually started to speak to him again. She told Pa he should fight the *goyishe* man in court because the *goyishe* man was wrong and Pa was right and it's a free country and we shouldn't let rich people run our lives. She said we should fight to the death, just like Paul Muni does in that movie, *I Am a Fugitive from a Chain Gang*. They send Paul to jail, Sophie said, but he never ever gives up. He even breaks out of prison. Sophie said we should be like Paul, and Pa should get a lawyer and fight, fight, fight.

But of course Ma and Pa have never ever been to any movie, and Pa didn't know what she was talking about. He told Sophie she was *meshugge* and made her mad at him all over again. It serves her right — she ought to know we can't afford a lawyer, especially now that the vegetable season is almost over and Pa has to look for other work again.

5693!

October 2

I'm going to write the date the Jewish way, too: 2 Tishrei 5693. It's Rosh Hashanah, so it's the year 5693 on the Jewish calendar now! Happy New Year! 5,693 is a lot more years than 1,932. We Jews have been around for a lot longer than the Christians have.

Anyway, I had so much fun yesterday. After we finished getting the house ready, me and Gert and the little ones put on our new outfits and went over to McCaul Street to the *shul*, like we do every year. All the girls go. We say we're just going to visit our mothers, but we all know the real reason is to show off our dresses to each other.

Of course, my new dress really isn't new. Gert had

it before me, and my cousin Humty had it before her and Dora had it before her and I think even Sophie had it once. But it's new to me, and Ma sewed a new pink ribbon around the neck that goes perfectly with the roses in the pattern. The girls at the *shul* said it looked adorable — even Rivka Goldstein, and she had a brand new dress of her very own, all in a silky material with a big bow at the waist. Rivka is so lucky to be the only girl in her family. I told everyone their dresses were adorable, too, but I really do think mine is the nicest. Except for Rivka's, of course.

Hindl was excited because her whole outfit was black — her dress, her socks, her shoes, and even her underpants — they were the ones Ma made out of an old cotton blouse Mrs. Feinblatt next door didn't want anymore. As soon as we got upstairs to where the ladies sit in the *shul*, Hindl ran up to Ma and said, "Look, Ma, everything matches," and she pulled up her skirt to show off her black underpants right in front of all the ladies! Ma pretended to be embarrassed and told Hindl to shush, but I could tell she really thought it was funny just like all the other ladies.

October 6

Rivka came over to visit after school. It was a real surprise. I mean, we're friends at school, and sometimes we walk home together because she lives just across the street, but golly, I hardly saw her all summer. I think she and her folks went to a cottage somewhere for a while. Pontypool, maybe. And anyway, I'm always busy with the little ones. It's hard to make time for friends when you have so many sisters that take up all your time. And when you have only one really old doll with no paint on its nose and almost no hair left. No wonder I don't like playing with dolls all that much.

Rivka must have been pleased I liked her new dress so much, because she let me borrow one of her Eaton's Beauty Dolls — she has three of them! She let me have Agatha, the one with blond hair and a beautiful yellow silk dress. I guess it was nice of her to let me play with Agatha, but still, Agatha is Rivka's oldest doll and Rivka made me pretend that Agatha was the maid for the other dolls. And she wouldn't even let my dolly Matilda be a maid. Rivka is nice, I guess, but she has no imagination.

Benny came over after supper. After spending two whole hours pretending to serve tea and cookies to Rivka's bossy dolls, I was happy to have someone sort of sensible to talk to.

Benny has another new job. It's at Woodbine Racetrack, of all places, and he won't tell me what it is. I bet it's because he's ashamed. What kind of job could there be at a racetrack that you shouldn't be ashamed of? Everyone knows that only *gonifs* and *trombeniks* and other criminals hang out at race-tracks.

At least he isn't talking about Germany so much anymore.

October 7

Another week is over, and Pa still can't find a job. There are signs all over saying *Jews Need Not Apply*, but Pa says he doesn't care, because he wouldn't work for people who weren't Jewish anyway. What he says he doesn't understand is why *Jewish* people can't find a job for him. Even if it is a Depression, Pa says, people should look after their own. Ma says he's right and he should ask one of her brothers for a job, but Pa won't do it. He says the Freedmans all look down on him because he's poor. They don't even care that he's a Cohen. Pa is so proud of being a Cohen because the Cohens are the tribe of priests and that should count for more than just money. But Uncle Bertzik and Uncle Velvel are Freedmans and it doesn't count to them.

Pa is spending a lot of time in the cellar, smoking and feeling sorry for himself. Ma won't let him smoke upstairs because it makes her feel nauseous and the smoke gets into the curtains, and now it's getting too cold for him to go outside. He's always here in the cellar when I want to write in my scribbler. The only reason I can do it right now is that it's Shabbes tonight and it's dark already and Pa's at the *shul*. I feel terrible about writing on Shabbes. I wish Pa would find a job.

October 10

It's so strange. Ma and Pa got so upset about Sophie and Steven because Steven wasn't Jewish and she was turning against her own religion. But I've been thinking about it a lot, and I hate to say it, but I'm starting to wonder why it even matters. I really do. Sophie's not a man, after all, and as far as I can tell, being religious is only important for men.

Sure, Ma does go to *shul* almost every Saturday. But usually all she does is sit up there on the second floor with the other women and knit and talk while the men are busy downstairs being religious and praying away like crazy. And they pray in Hebrew, of course, and none of us can understand Hebrew except Pa. Not even Ma — she just knows Yiddish and a little bit of English, because she's a lady and not a man. Only boys go to *cheder* to learn Hebrew after regular school because only boys have to learn how to pray.

Except for praying over the candles on Shabbes, of course, and that's easy. I've never actually done it myself, but I've heard Ma do it so often I bet I could learn to do it in about ten minutes if I had to.

So why does it really matter if Sophie marries a *goy*?

Pa sure thinks it does. He says we should stick to our own kind, and I guess he's right. And I do like being Jewish. When Ma lights the candles on Shabbes it makes me feel so peaceful. And it would be horrible being something else and having to eat bacon and other *trayf* all the time.

Sometimes life is so confusing.

Or maybe I'm just confused because it's Yom Kippur today and we aren't supposed to eat anything all day long because it's the day of atonement and we have to make up for all the bad things we did in the last year by not eating. I don't know exactly how not eating helps. It just makes my head hurt. I guess it's like being punished, and I guess I deserve it this year. I really should have told Ma and Pa about Sophie and Steven. What was I thinking?

Ma says we can have something to eat if we get really hungry, because the important thing is that we tried. But she never ever eats anything on Yom Kippur, and neither do Sophie or Dora, so I'm not going to either. At least not before Gert does.

That's why I snuck down here to write in my scribbler, to keep my mind off my headache and my empty tummy. But now Gert is calling me to come to the *shul* with her. She wants to stand outside on the steps after the service and say, "I wish I never knew you" real fast to all the grown-ups as they walk past. She says they'll think she's saying, "I wish you a happy new year." I hope they do, or Pa will be furious.

October 11

When Gert told the grown-ups she wished she never knew them, they just smiled and said, "The same to you, darling." Gert thought it proved how clever she was for tricking them. I was about to tell her that they were really saying they wished they never knew *her*, either, right back — but I was smart enough to keep my mouth shut for once. Sometimes I wish I never knew Gert.

On the way home from *shul* I met Benny on the street. He was walking over to Spadina to get a corned beef sandwich! And he asked me if I wanted to come and get one, too! On Yom Kippur!

I guess it's not surprising that Benny is such a bad Jew. His pa is, too. Benny says it's because Uncle Max is a socialist and socialists don't believe in silly superstitions and want to make the world a better place. Pa says it's because Uncle Max is a no-good drunk and a *gonif* and a gambler.

Benny wouldn't even have learned Hebrew if his ma hadn't got sick last year while his pa had gone off somewhere and didn't come home for a long time. Nobody knows where Uncle Max went to this day. He's been doing strange things like that ever since he came back from the war, Ma says.

Anyway, that was when the lady came from the Jewish Children's Aid and took Benny and Willie and Joe and put them in the Jewish orphanage because his older brothers and sisters couldn't afford to look after them. While Benny was in the orphanage, the people there found out he never went to *shul* and that he wasn't learning the prayers he had to say for a *bar mitzvah* even though he was almost thirteen already. Benny told them that none of his older brothers had a *bar mitzvah* and he wasn't going to either, but they made him go to a rabbi to learn the prayers anyway. Benny says that the rabbi's beard smelled awful, like mothballs, and the rabbi hit him over the knuckles with a big stick whenever he got the prayers wrong, which was all the time. Benny got *bar-mitzvahed*, all right, but he says it was enough religion for him for the rest of his life.

Poor Benny. I guess I understand. But still, that doesn't mean he has to tempt people with corned-beef sandwiches on Yom Kippur. And he shouldn't go around forcing people to listen to his awful stories from the newspaper about how the Nazis want to kill all the Jews because they believe Jews kill Christian children and mix their blood into cakes to eat at Passover. That's too awful to think about it. How can people believe such terrible lies and even put them in the newspaper for other people to read and pass on? I like Benny, but sometimes he makes me so angry.

October 13

Pa went to the court yesterday because of the accident, and he ended up in jail! Imagine — my pa, in jail with all the crooks and bad people. Pa is a Cohen! It's awful even just thinking about it, even if he was only there for a few hours.

Pa went by himself. Sophie tried to get him to let her come and translate for him but he said it was no place for a good Jewish woman. I bet he's sorry he said that now.

Pa said the judge listened to what the *goyishe* man with the big limousine said. Then he told Pa he had to pay a fine without even listening to Pa's side of the story. Pa said he tried to tell the judge he was blowing the horn while he was driving the truck onto the highway, so it really wasn't his fault and he shouldn't have to pay the fine. But I guess Pa's English wasn't good enough, because the judge thought Pa was saying he wouldn't pay ever at all and so he told the policemen there to throw Pa into jail. So they did. Pa says it never would have happened in the old country. Of course it wouldn't. Pa never had a truck in the old country.

They let Pa make a phone call, but of course we can't afford a phone anymore, so he called Mrs. Koslov at the grocery store up the street and she sent her horrible son Irving down to say that Pa was in the Don Jail and we had to bring money to pay the fine before they would let him out. That blabbermouth Irving told everyone he passed on the way here and so now everyone on the block knows all about it. Even Rivka Goldstein, and she'll tell all the girls at school. I could kill him.

Everyone else was at work, so Ma and me and the little ones had to walk over to Spadina to the factory and get the money from Uncle Bertzik. Hindl complained it was too far, but Molly didn't say anything. After we walked right through the factory with everyone staring at us — even Sophie and Dora and Gert — we found Uncle Bertzik in his office. He got mad at Ma and made her cry, but he finally gave her the money. Then Ma made me go on the streetcar all the way to the Don Jail with it to get Pa out.

Pa wasn't happy about that, but what else could Ma do? I guess she could have pawned some things, like Benny's ma always does — Ma still has the nice silver necklace her pa gave her when she got married. But Pa would have been even angrier about that. Pa says only weaklings and *gonifs* go to pawnshops, not good Jews.

I had to go on the streetcar by myself because we couldn't afford the extra carfares and anyway, Ma couldn't speak to the people in the jail in English and I can. I wish she could, too. Pa is right. It's no place for a good Jewish girl.

When I got there, it was such a huge building, and I couldn't figure out where to go, so I asked a policeman who was standing there how to get inside. He said, "Hit a policeman," and he started to laugh. I was so mad at him that I almost did hit a policeman. But after he stopped laughing, he took me inside to the right place and I gave the man there the money and they let Pa out. Pa was still furious. He jabbered away in Yiddish on the streetcar all the way home. Everyone was staring at us.

October 14

Miss Douglas gave us all poems to memorize today. I wanted to do "Lady Moon, Lady Moon, where are you roving?" because it's so, so romantic, but she gave that to one of the boys and made me take "Little Girls" by a lady poet named Laurence Alma-Tedema. It starts out like this:

If no one ever marries me
And I don't see why they should
For nurse says I'm not pretty
And I'm seldom very good.

If I have to recite that in front of the whole class I'll just die.

October 17

We are so broke now it isn't funny. It was bad enough before the court fine, but it's even worse now, and Pa won't even let Ma go ask Uncle Bertzik for some help because he's so angry and embarrassed about Uncle Bertzik paying the fine. But the worst thing is, Miss Douglas told us last week that we should be thinking of all the poor people suffering from the Depression and she wanted everyone to bring a penny to help people less well off than ourselves, and of course we don't have any pennies to spare. When Miss Douglas passed the jar today I said I didn't bring a penny, but I didn't tell her why. It's none of her business. Miss Douglas was very angry. She said it looked like she'd have to put one of her own pennies in the jar for Sally Cohen, and she did. She said it in a very loud voice so everyone in the whole class could hear.

I used to think Miss Douglas was nice, but now I don't. That was a mean thing to do. And she says I have to recite "Little Girls" this week.

October 19

Everyone is so unhappy. Pa has no job and no money and Ma is worried all the time, and we never get anything to eat but eggs and potatoes and porridge and Sophie is still doing nothing but getting mad at Pa and moping about that awful Steven. At least she still goes to the factory.

I am unhappy because I am worried about everybody, but especially about Benny. I don't know why I care, but I do. Benny finally told me what he's doing at the racetrack. He says he's a table.

That's right. A table. Like what you eat on. Benny says there are men under the stands — where the people sit to watch the races — who take bets on the horses. They're called bookies, but it has nothing to do with reading. Benny says it's against the law to be a bookie, so they hire boys like him to stand there and hold open a newspaper, so it's flat. Like a table. The bookie does whatever they do with money and things on top of the newspaper. Then, if someone says the police are coming, the table folds up the newspaper with all the money still inside it and pretends to be just a paperboy — which Benny really is. He got the table job from a man he was selling a paper to every day on College Street outside of Altman's.

Benny says he makes a lot of money being a table. He even offered me two whole dollars. That's a fortune, and I almost took it because we need it so much. But then I remembered where the money came from and I said no, never in a million years. Benny should know better. I tried to get him to stop being a table but he just laughed. What if he gets caught?

The only good thing is that my flannel underpants are finally done. The seams are crooked, but maybe Ma can fix them. Thank goodness. I hope the next thing we make in Domestic Science isn't so private.

October 21

Miss Douglas made me say my poem today. I did it really, really fast and I pretended to forget the part about not being pretty. Everyone could tell Miss Douglas was angry, but I don't care. No one's going to make me say I'm not pretty in front of everybody even if I'm not. It's almost Shabbes, so that's all for now.

October 26

I haven't written anything in this scribbler for a while because it's so hard to write. My hands are like ice. Sophie says the radio says it's warmer than average, but still, the house is getting chilly now and the furnace isn't on because Pa says we can't afford the coal. The only warm place is beside the stove in the kitchen where I do my homework. But today I decided to sneak down to the cellar and get my scribbler and bring it up here to my room so I can get under the covers and write. If anyone comes in I'll just say it's homework.

My winter blanket is so itchy. It's the patchwork one that Ma made out of the greatcoat Uncle Bertzik wore in the Great War, but it always makes me think of Uncle Max, not Uncle Bertzik. I guess that's because Uncle Bertzik is a *mensch*. Even though he owns a factory and he's very rich, he just seems like everyone else.

Although, come to think of it, I guess Uncle Bertzik isn't really a *mensch*. He refuses to help out Benny's ma just because he hates Uncle Max — that's no way to treat your very own sister.

But Uncle Max is a whole different story. He got gassed in the war and had some of his toes shot off. I've never seen his feet and I never want to. Anyway, Benny says that's why his pa acts so crazy all the time. But Pa says Max was always a *trombenik*. He was making trouble even back in the old country before he married Auntie Esther, long before the war.

Once last year I overheard Pa and Ma in the summer kitchen talking about when Uncle Max got drafted into the Russian army back in the old country. Pa said Uncle Max just ran away in the night with his brother's papers without telling anybody, and his poor brother, Benny's Uncle Peretz, had to go and serve in his place. Auntie Esther was already married to Uncle Max then, and they had Sam and Al and another child on the way — Ruthie, who is twenty-two now. But Uncle Max just left them with no money or anything and ran off to Canada.

Auntie Esther didn't let him get away with it. She packed up a bag and took the children and walked miles and miles to where she could get on a boat and come to Canada and find him. They got together again, and that's when Rosie and Benny and Willie and Joe came along. And then Uncle Max ended up being in the Canadian army and being in the war anyway and losing his toes. Serves him right.

Pa thinks Auntie Esther was *meshugge* for even wanting to find Uncle Max again and so does Uncle Bertzik. But I think it's romantic. I wish I could be as brave as Auntie Esther.

I'll never tell Benny about Uncle Max running away. Maybe it wouldn't bother Benny, but if anything like that ever happened to my parents, I would honestly rather just not know. Anyway, I'm sure it didn't. Ma and Pa knew each other in the old country, even though they didn't get married until they came to Canada. But Pa would never run away. I'm lucky to have a pa like Pa — he's a good pa even if he is a little strict sometimes. I wish he would find a job and b

November 9

The last time I wrote in this scribbler I had a really close call. Gert came in to get a sweater and I had to stop writing right in the middle of a sentence and hide it under the covers and I've been afraid to try to write anything since then. But today it seemed warm enough to come down here to the cellar again, even if the furnace isn't on. Maybe I'm just getting used to being cold.

There's nothing much to write, really. I'm just going to school and looking after Molly and Hindl and doing the usual things I always do. I've hardly even seen Benny. He just came over once to tell me about how thousands and thousands of children marched for Hitler in Germany. I think he just comes over here to tell me scary things and make me mad, and the rest of the time he hangs out with some boys he knows from the track. Some of them aren't even Jewish. I hope he knows what he's doing.

I hate to admit it, but sometimes I wish I could go to the track, or golly, to anywhere interesting. Sure, school is okay, but it's kind of boring. I like learning things, of course. I just wish it didn't take so long.

I played dolls with Rivka again, on Sunday. My doll still had to be the maid and Rivka wouldn't let Molly join in even though she really wanted to and she just sat there and didn't say anything and watched us the whole time and I was so glad when Rivka finally went home. I wonder what it's like to be at the track.

Pa still doesn't have a job. We've been living for weeks now on loans from Uncle Bertzik and on what Sophie and Dora and Gert make, which is next to nothing, and I'm always so cold. But at least it's warm at school — especially in Domestic Science now that we're cooking instead of sewing. We made blanc-mange last week. It tasted okay, but a little boring.

I almost forgot. Everything isn't boring. Last week I got into big trouble, and it was all because I like to read. Life is so unfair. I was putting the dishes away after supper, and I noticed that one of the pieces of old newspaper Ma got from Mrs. Koslov to use as shelf paper had comics on it. So I climbed on a chair to read them. But while I was reading I accidentally pushed a box of matches off the shelf, and they fell into the *schmaltz* Ma was making from the chicken fat Auntie Rayzel gave her. I got them out right away, but Ma was really upset anyway, because she didn't know if the *schmaltz* was still going to be kosher after matches fell into it. Pa didn't know either. He had to take the pot to the *shul* and ask the Rabbi. The Rabbi said it would be okay, thank goodness. He even stamped it with his *hechsher* to show it was kosher.

November 13

It was Shabbes yesterday, and a funny thing happened. It started when I heard "Stardust" playing real loud on the radio, so I went into the parlour to sing along. I was pretending to be an opera singer like I always do and singing in as high a voice as I could when Benny walked in and started singing in a high voice, too, to tease me. I nearly died.

Sometimes I wish Benny didn't like me. He doesn't like any of my sisters, that's for sure, which means he never teases them. He just avoids them as much as he can. But he teases me all the time and then he laughs like crazy when I get mad. I think he just likes making me mad.

The most annoying thing is, I kind of *like* getting mad at him. It's — well, it's interesting. It's ever so much more interesting than being yelled at by Gert or helping Molly do everything or pretending to serve imaginary biscuits to Rivka's doll Agatha.

After Benny stopped laughing, he told me his job at the track was over and he's back to selling papers. I guess it's better than being arrested. But it means I'll be hearing about Germany all the time again. Darn. He also joined a Greco-Roman wrestling club. That's the right way to spell it because I asked him and he told me. He's going to be in a demonstration at the Labour Lyceum over on Spadina, and he invited me to come. He says he was thinking about boxing, but wrestling is more artistic — whatever that means. I think he's just afraid of getting punched.

Anyway, the radio was playing so loud we almost couldn't hear each other. Benny suddenly stopped talking right in the middle of a sentence and went over and turned it off, and right away, Sophie came rushing in and she was furious. She was sitting in the kitchen leafing through a *Time* magazine Syd loaned her and listening and of course, once the radio was turned off we couldn't turn it back on because it was Shabbes. On Fridays Pa lets us leave it on and we can turn the volume up or down, but once it's off, it's off. Benny said it wasn't a big deal and turned it on again. That made Sophie even angrier, but you could tell she was happy about being able to listen again. She even talked to us a little bit. But not for long. I wish she would stop being such a mope. She hasn't been the same since Pa said she couldn't get married.

After Sophie left, I told Benny that of course I couldn't go to the wrestling. What was he thinking? I'm a girl. Ma and Pa would never allow it. Anyway, Pa would never let me go to the Labour Lyceum. He says that it's just a bunch of godless communists in there, thinking they're so clever and making trouble for the rest of us.

November 18

Ma is so angry at Pa because of what he did to her yesterday. Ma said she thought she heard something making a noise in the cellar, and it might be a mouse, so she sent Pa down to look. When he came back, he was holding his hanky, and there was a long thin brown thing hanging out of it, just like a mouse's tail. He held it up to Ma's face and said, "Look what I found," and she screamed and nearly fainted. But then Pa unwrapped his hanky and there was nothing but a beet inside. He laughed like crazy till Ma started yelling at him.

Pa is usually so serious. Is being out of work driving him crazy?

November 21

Pa finally got a job. I am so relieved.

The job is on the assembly line at Christie's Biscuits. Pa puts arrowroot biscuits into boxes and he hates it, but at least we're going to get something to eat besides the beets and potatoes we have left in the cellar from last fall. Ma said she'll even buy a chicken on Thursday for Shabbes. We haven't had one for so long, I can hardly remember what it tastes like.

November 24

Ma made me go with her after school to buy the chicken. When we got to Baldwin Street, I waited outside the cage while Ma went in and caught one. There were three other ladies in the cage, too, and about a dozen chickens. It was funny to watch them chasing around in there. I couldn't help laughing.

Ma must have noticed, though, because after she paid for the chicken, she put it in the baby carriage she uses for shopping and made me take it to the *shochet* while she went home. She knows how much I hate going to the *shochet*. His shed is so tiny, and you have to stand real close while he slits the chickens' throats with his knife and then sticks their poor little heads in the hole in the trough to drain the blood and make them kosher. Sometimes the chickens give a little cluck even after they're in the holes. Sometimes they actually pull their heads out of the holes and fly up at you. It's a truly awful place. Sometimes I have nightmares about it.

I still like chicken, though, and I can hardly wait to have some tomorrow. It's been such a long, long time since the last chicken. I'm such a terrible person, I really am.

We didn't have enough money to get one of the ladies who work at the *shochet's* to pluck the chicken. Ma is doing it herself out in the summer kitchen right now.

November 26

The chicken was delicious last night. I feel awful about it.

November 30

Today in school Miss Douglas was upset because Meyer Eckel was absent again — he hasn't been there for almost two weeks now. Miss Douglas got a snooty look on her face and said it was hardly surprising that certain kinds of people don't manage to get ahead when they can't even get themselves out of bed to come to school and get an education. I hate to admit it, but I think that when she said certain kinds of people she meant Jews, because she also said it would never happen with a boy of good British stock. I think Miss Douglas is an *anti-semit.* It makes me mad.

It's strange, though, because most of the time she seems to like me. She's always telling the others how clever I am and embarrassing me. Last week she said that there were two wonderfully gifted writers in the class, and one was me and the other was Myrtle MacDonald. I don't understand people at all.

Anyway, Miss Douglas was wrong about Meyer Eckel. Later, on the playground at recess, I heard Hannah Klipstein tell some other girls that Meyer was her cousin and the reason he wasn't coming to school was that his shoes had worn through and his father is out of work and they can't afford new ones. It must be true, because when he was coming Meyer always wore the same filthy shirt with holes in it. I never noticed his shoes. Who ever looks at other people's feet?

After I heard about the shoes, I was even angrier at Miss Douglas. I'm tempted to tell Benny, even though he'll say I told you so.

I wonder what kind of stories Myrtle MacDonald writes.

December 4

I am so angry at Benny. I am never talking to him ever again.

He came over because he couldn't think of anything else to do. He was very bored, and he said it was all because of the *goyim*. Sunday is their Shabbes, and so they make sure that nothing is open, no stores or restaurants or anything. There's nowhere to go and nothing to do.

Benny is right. It is boring. They even tie up the swings in the playgrounds so you can't go and swing. And they pull the drapes on the windows at Eaton's so you can't look at the Christmas windows, which is sad because I love those windows even if Christmas isn't Jewish and anyway, it's mostly just elves and princesses from fairy tales, not anything really religious.

Anyway, Benny talked me into going out for a walk with him, even though there was really nowhere to go. I didn't want to go because I had to wear my new coat. It's the only one that fits. My old one wasn't all that small, but Ma gave it to Auntie Bella for my cousin Millie's cousin Freda on the other side.

I hate the new coat. No matter what Ma says, a reefer coat is a boy's coat, and anyone who takes even a little teensy look at it will know that it's a boy's coat. I wish my cousin Manny hadn't grown two whole inches in a year so that the coat doesn't fit him anymore and Auntie Rayzel had to hand it down to me. He probably just grew like that to annoy me.

I had a very embarrassing experience because of that coat. And because of Benny.

I wore the coat when I went out with him, but I pulled my stocking hat down as far as it would go so no one would recognize me. After Benny and I walked around for a while we got really cold, so he suggested we go to St. Christopher House. It's open on Sundays and they let you in out of the cold if you're willing to colour Bible pictures. I think we're both much too old for colouring and I told him so, too, but Benny talked me into it because his coat isn't as warm as mine and he was freezing.

When we got there, the lady looked at me in my coat and hat and said, "May I help you, sonny?" She really did. She called me sonny. I was furious, absolutely furious.

Benny just laughed. He laughed for a long, long time. But then he got a strange look in his eye and he snapped his fingers and he said, "That's it!"

Benny told me he figures that I can sneak into the wrestling exhibition wearing my reefer coat and stocking hat, and no one will ever suspect I'm a girl.

I am devastated and humiliated and deeply, deeply upset. What a terrible insult! I left Benny right there in St. Chris by himself and came right home and I am never ever talking to him again.

December 10

I'm so glad Pa's working now. He's so much happier and nicer to everybody. And I like the broken arrowroot biscuits he brings home. This week, there was enough money for Ma to buy an *Amerikaner* magazine. She hasn't been able to get one for months and months. This morning, she let me curl up in her bed with her while she read me the stories from the magazine in Yiddish — just like I loved to do when I was little.

December 12

I am such a softie. I actually talked to Benny today. I even agreed to his stupid idea about the coat and the wrestling.

It was because he came over to apologize to me with a big bruise on his cheek. I thought it was from wrestling but he said it was because his pa was on the warpath again. Benny's brother Al got Benny a job in the belt factory where he works, and Uncle Max told him he had to take it or else he'd throw him out of the house. Benny said fine, he'd go, he didn't want to live there anyway, so Uncle Max gave him a big slap. But afterwards, Benny remembered he had nowhere to go to and it's too cold out now to just stay on the street or sleep on our front porch and he didn't want to end up like all those other boys who sneak rides on the railways and go all across the country and have no home at all. So he's working at the belt factory. He cuts out belts and the machine has a huge sharp knife in it and the leather is very stiff and hard to cut.

It sounds awful. Benny looked so sad I couldn't help myself. I said I'd go to the wrestling.

What was I thinking of? Lady Flora Eaton would never dress up like a boy. It's not ladylike.

I can't decide whether I hope people think I'm a

boy or find out I'm a girl and kick me out. Either way, it will be awful. Maybe I'll just pretend to be too sick to go.

December 13

I'm so excited. Today, Miss Douglas announced that a lady named Miss Tedde is coming to our school to listen to us all sing. She's going to pick the people who sing the best to be in a big choir of children from schools all over the whole city. It's my big chance to start my opera career! Miss Tedde will be so proud of me when I sing at the Metropolitan Opera some day, and so will Ma and Pa. I've been practising by singing "Stardust" all evening. I can get my voice ever so high.

December 14

I went to the wrestling demonstration. I told Benny I couldn't go because I had a bad cold, but he didn't believe me. He grabbed my hand and dragged me out onto the porch before I could do anything about it. He wouldn't even let me go back in to get my hat and coat. He went back in and got them for me and I had to put them on out there. It was below zero and I was freezing.

It's so strange. I've been going to school and the

market and everywhere in the reefer coat and the stocking hat for almost two weeks now and I just felt dumb because everyone would think I was a boy and I didn't want them to. But last night I wanted them to, and it was exciting, like I was wearing a disguise or I was a spy or something.

I shouldn't be excited by things like that. It isn't refined. I'm afraid Benny knows me better than I think.

I was worried that people would think it was strange for me to keep my hat and coat on even if they did think I was a boy. But Benny said that nowadays a lot of men keep their coats on at meetings and things because they're too poor to buy new shirts and suits and they don't want people to see how awful their clothes look. He was right, too. Nobody at the Labour Lyceum even noticed me at all.

Life is so confusing. How will I ever get to be a famous opera singer if people can't tell I'm not a boy? Still, it's a good thing they couldn't — for today, at least.

The demonstration was awful. Boys or men came out two at a time and got down on the floor and held each other in strange positions and grunted for a while, and then they got up and everyone clapped and they went away and two more came. The wrestlers were wearing hardly any clothes at all, and none of them seemed to be the least bit embarrassed. I sure am glad I'm not really a boy.

Benny was looking even skinnier than last summer at the Ex. He must be ever so hungry. Still, he almost won his demonstration, but then the other boy twisted in a funny way and Benny had to give up. He *kvetched* about it all the way home.

After the wrestling exhibition, Benny talked me into going to Altman's for a soda. I've never been there before. Pa would kill me if he found out. I feel awful about it, but I have to admit that it was exciting being there, too. It's hard to believe the world is so different just a few blocks from my own house.

There were lots of men and boys in Altman's, smoking and *kibitzing* and eating pickles and sandwiches, and they all knew Benny and said hi to him when we walked in. He told them I was his cousin Mendel from Sarnia. I just sat there and didn't say anything and tried to look invisible. They talked about gambling and where to buy illegal liquor and they said simply awful things about ladies, especially certain parts of ladies' bodies that I can't write down. It makes me blush to even think of them, and I'm so glad I don't have any yet. I blushed in Altman's when I heard the men talk about them, and one of the men teased me and said they sure do make the boys green in Sarnia and told me I should stop being such a little girlie. If he only knew.

December 15

Today was the most embarrassing and awful day of my whole entire life. I hate myself. I hate my stupid voice. I hate Miss Tedde.

Miss Tedde made everybody sing for a bit, and then she stopped them and said, "Thank you, dear," and sent them back to their seats. But when my turn came, she didn't say thank you. She just gave me a strange look and said, "Hmm, I really don't know, dear. Would you mind singing again?" So I sang again — and Miss Tedde did the same thing again. She did it three whole times. I don't know why she did it, I really don't. If she didn't like my voice, why didn't she just stop me and go on to someone else? Finally I couldn't stand it anymore. I burst into tears right there in front of everybody and I shouted at Miss Tedde. I said, "If you don't want me, why don't you say so?" And I ran out of the room crying like crazy.

Miss Douglas came and got me and told me I was being over-emotional and wiped my face with her hanky and made me go back into the classroom. Everyone was staring at me and laughing at me behind my back, I just know they were.

I don't know what Miss Tedde was so confused about. I was singing in a lovely high voice. Nobody else sang anywhere near as high as I did.

I hate music. I am never going to sing another note again in my entire life.

December 22

They had Christmas carols at St. Christopher House tonight. I went last year and the year before, but of course I'm not going this year, because I'm never ever singing ever again. You couldn't drag me there with a team of horses. I'm sorry I won't get to see the Christmas tree because it's always ever so lovely even if it isn't Jewish, and of course the carols aren't Jewish, either. I guess that's one good thing about not singing. It will make me a better Jew. Although I guess I won't be singing any Hanukkah songs either.

December 25

I couldn't help myself. I sang "Dreidel Dreidel Dreidel" right along with everyone else after supper tonight. But that's it. I'm never singing again.

December 26

It was so hot yesterday! The radio said it was a record high, 57°! The announcer said people were wading in Etobicoke Creek and it didn't feel at all like Christmas.

Speaking of Christmas, Pa was mad at Auntie Esther today because of it. She was over for tea and told Ma she put Willie and Joe on the list for the *Star* Santa Claus Fund. Really! She did! And on Saturday they got the boxes! There was a new sweater and stockings and mittens and candies and an orange for each of them, and Willie got a toy truck and Joe got a ball. Pa says that accepting charity from *goyim* is bad enough, but even worse, what did Willie and Joe need with Christmas presents of all things? What kind of Jews get Christmas presents? It would never happen in the old country.

Pa's probably right. But I have to admit I'm kind of sorry about it, because last week I heard on the radio that all the girls' boxes have a talking Mama Doll in them this year. I don't like dolls all that much, but I bet Rivka wouldn't make a talking doll be a maid.

December 28

Yesterday, Gert whined at Ma for hours and hours so she could go to a movie with her friend

Ida. They wanted to go to the College Theatre on College Street and see Douglas Fairbanks in *Mr. Robinson Crusoe*. Douglas Fairbanks is very handsome for an old man. Ma said Gert could go but only if she took me along because I was moping around the house with nothing to do and getting in her hair. Gert agreed and asked Ma for money, and Ma said she only had 10¢ and would that do, and Gert said it'd be enough for both of us. But when we got there, it was 10¢ *each*. The College Theatre is so expensive, and Gert knew it was all along. She is so mean.

Gert told me I had to stand there and wait in the lobby while she went in with Ida and saw the movie. I was so furious I almost started to walk home by myself even though it was pitch black out and there might be hoboes or other bad men around and I was kind of scared. But then Mrs. Koslov from the grocery store showed up and asked why I was there and lent me the money to get in. I took the 10¢, but only after Mrs. Koslov promised not to tell Ma. If Ma found out she'd be mad at Gert and then Gert would be mad at me. Ten whole cents! I don't know how I'll ever pay it back.

The movie was okay, I guess, but I was so mad at Gert I wasn't really paying attention. All the way home I walked behind her and kept stepping onto the backs of her shoes and saying it was an accident. It made me feel much better.

December 30

Benny is in a band now. It's completely ridiculous, because he doesn't know anything about music and he can't sing and he can't play any musical instrument. All he has is a white tuxedo.

It's a used tuxedo, and it fits Benny perfectly. He showed it to me. He looks very elegant in it. Benny's ma found it on a table in front of a second-hand store on Kensington and it was really cheap so she bought it. Auntie Esther is always finding bargains. She's so poor I guess she has to, just like us — but sometimes the bargains she finds aren't very practical.

Since he already had the suit, Benny got Harvey Tischler and some of his other friends who play instruments together and they formed a band. They call themselves Ben Applebaum and the Sons of Rhythm. Since Benny has the tuxedo, he's the band-leader, and he waves a stick around while the other boys play. Benny says he has no idea what he's doing, but the boys in the band just try not to watch him too much and it sounds all right.

Benny gets to be in a band without even playing,

while I have to give up music forever because of that crazy Miss Tedde. Life is so unfair.

1933

January 1, 1933

Happy New Year! When you're Jewish, you're lucky enough to get a new year twice a year. Or maybe it's not so lucky, because you get older twice as fast? Or maybe my head is filled with crazy ideas just because I'm just bored and can't wait for school to start again.

January 4

Gert is being very nice to me now — for Gert. Somehow Dora found out about the movies. I wonder if Mrs. Koslov told her. Anyway, Dora took Gert aside and talked to her about it, and Gert told her she was sorry and I think she is, but because of Dora, not because of me. Even Gert can't help being nice to Dora, and so she's trying to be nicer to me. Thank heavens for Dora.

After the holiday, Meyer Eckel came back to school with new shoes but the same old shirt. Miss Douglas wasn't very nice to him about staying away for so long and said he might fail the grade. But at least he's there to try. Hannah says the shoes came from the *Star* Santa Claus Fund. Maybe it isn't so bad for Jews to get Christmas presents after all.

January 8

We have a guest staying in the house with us. It's Pa's second cousin, Yankl, from Saskatchewan.

He looked awful when he came, just awful. He was covered with grimy black soot, and his clothes were ripped and torn and he looked like he needed a shave and a haircut. And he smelled really bad, like he hadn't had a bath in a year. When Ma and I answered the doorbell, she thought he was just another hobo looking for a handout, and she told me to tell him we didn't have anything to give him and he should go away. I wish she would learn some English so I don't always have to go to the door and translate for her. But I didn't have to translate this time, because he started talking in Yiddish! He said, "Reva, don't you remember me?" and Ma took a closer look and realized who he was. She knew him from when she was just my age, back in the old country, and he came here once years ago when he first came to Canada. He's a lot younger than Pa, but he and Pa were always together, Ma says, more like friends than like cousins. Just like me and Benny, Ma says.

Anyway, Yankl looked a lot different after Ma poured him a bath and lent him some of Pa's clothes. For one thing, he was a lot skinnier. He told us he looked so fat before because he was wearing all of his clothes at the same time — two shirts, two pairs of pants, a sweater, a jacket and a coat!

He was wearing all his clothes because he has been riding the rails! He came all the way from Regina by stealing rides in boxcars on trains! No wonder he was dirty! And so hungry, too — he gulped down so many potatoes! Ma kept giving him another helping, and he kept shoving them in. He must have been starving.

Now he's upstairs sleeping in my room, and Gert and I have to go sleep upstairs in the attic with Sophie and Dora. Sophie and Dora are sharing one of the beds, and Gert and I will share the other one.

January 9

I had a horrible night. Gert hogged all the space and hit me when she rolled over too far. It was truly awful. It's a good thing that Yankl is here for only a few days. He's on his way to see his sister in Montreal.

He's going there because he can't find any work in Saskatchewan. It's so sad. He told Ma and Pa he had a farm near a place in Saskatchewan called Wapella, but he lost it two years ago after there was a drought and the wind blew the soil away and he had a bad crop — and anyway, he says, the price of wheat was so low he didn't even make enough money from selling the wheat to pay for growing it. He says he and his wife had to live for most of that winter on jackrabbits they caught and Russian thistle, which is a kind of weed that Yankl says grows like crazy even when the wheat won't. His wife was expecting a baby and I guess not eating very much made her sick, because both she and the baby died before it could be born. He cried when he told us about it.

Yankl gave up the farm after that, and ever since then he's been going from farm to farm in Saskatchewan looking for work. Sometimes people had small jobs for him to do, but mostly, they couldn't afford to hire him and he had to beg for food to keep alive. He figured if he could get to Montreal his sister could help him and maybe get him a job in her husband's delicatessen or something — but he never got enough money together to afford a train ticket. Then he was in a soup kitchen in Regina a few weeks ago and a man he met there said he was heading that way and Yankl could come with him. Yankl figured he was too old and weak to ride the rails, and he was afraid of slipping under the car while he was jumping to get on it and being run over. But this man said he'd help him, and Yankl decided he had nothing to lose, and that's how he ended up riding the rails.

He says riding the rails was no fun at all, and he did nearly slip and fall under the train. He also got chased by the "bulls" a couple of times — that's what he calls the railway police, and he says they're really mean and they like to beat up hoboes. And once he was on a coal-and-water car and a railway worker saw him and turned a hose on him and the water pushed him right off the train. No wonder he looked so awful. He says he had all his clothes on when he came because it's really hard to jump onto a moving train if you're carrying a bag or anything. Those ratty clothes are everything he owns in the whole world — except for a wrinkled-up picture of his wife he keeps in his pocket all the time.

Ma and Pa tried to talk him into staying for a while, but he said no. He's going to leave tomorrow. I guess he could tell we really couldn't afford to keep him for long. And he wouldn't let Pa give him a little money towards getting a ticket to Montreal.

January 11

Yankl has gone. He put all his own clothes back on and left. Ma tried to clean up the clothes, but they're so old and torn they didn't really look all that different. I'm glad to get my own bed back, but I sure hope Yankl makes it to Montreal in one piece. He is kind of sad all the time, but he's a nice man.

Now that she knows about Yankl, I hope that Sophie won't say such mean things about hoboes anymore. It's not his fault if he's poor.

January 15

I was a boy again yesterday. Benny sweet-talked me into doing it, and I'm almost getting used to it. The Gelman brothers knew someone who knew someone who needed a band for a dance, so they took the job, and they needed a person to help Harvey Tischler carry all his drums on the streetcar. The boys in the band knew I was a girl, of course, but they made me keep my coat and hat on in case anyone at the dance complained about me being with them.

Harvey Tischler is all right, I guess, but I hate being around him. He always smells so bad. Benny says it's because Harvey loves playing street hockey. The boys use frozen horse manure for a puck. I think it's disgusting, but Benny says, what else can they do if they can't afford a real puck? Anyway, whenever Harvey sees a good horse ball on the street, he puts it in his pocket to bring home and keep on the porch for the next game. But they always melt a little in his pocket on the way home, which is why he always smells. Benny says the boys call him Harvey the Horseballer. Boys are so strange. I used to think it was just Benny.

The dance was in a Church of England church. Benny didn't tell me before we got there, because if he had, then of course I wouldn't have gone. I've never been in a church before. Sure, I guess St. Chris is sort of churchy, but it's right on our street and it just seems like home. I've been going there forever, and they never preach or pray if you don't count the Bible pictures they have for kids to colour. It felt strange being there, and I hope Pa never finds out.

Considering they've hardly ever rehearsed together or anything, the band was pretty good. The Gelman brothers are great on the fiddle and the sax, and Harv makes a lot of noise with the drums, and Benny looks very handsome in his tuxedo. You can't even tell how skinny he is. They played "Stardust" and I started to hum along without even realizing it, and had to make myself stop. It's the very last time I will ever sing.

January 18

So much schoolwork! I never seem to have any time to write anything here. Anyway, there isn't much to write about. Just the same old routine.

We did get a letter last week from my Uncle Izzy, Pa's youngest brother. The letter had such an interesting stamp on it, because Uncle Izzy lives in the old country — in Riga, which is the capital city of Latvia. But the stamp said *Latvija* instead of Latvia — I guess because it's written in Latvian.

Uncle Izzy came to live in Canada once, and he stayed here in the house with us. It was back when I was really, really young, and I can't remember him at all. But Dora says he had a different prayer for everything he did all day long — he even had one for tying his shoes! And Gert says he hogged the toilet room and made it very stinky. She should talk. Anyway, she says she wasn't the least bit sorry when Uncle Izzy decided he didn't like it in Canada and went back to Latvia.

Pa says Uncle Izzy didn't like Canada because nobody here cares about Cohens and nobody has any respect for the old ways. Pa says he sometimes feels the same way.

But Sophie says that what Uncle Izzy really didn't like was that nobody ever listened to him here in Canada. She says he was a real sourpuss who thought he knew everything, and she bets he isn't happy in Latvia either. She says Uncle Izzy wouldn't be happy even if rabbis ruled the world and made all the girls wear skirts down to their ankles all the time.

When he was in Canada, Uncle Izzy must have made some really mean comments about Sophie's skirts. She's still mad at him all these years later.

Uncle Izzy says he's married now, so I have a new auntie! He sounds very happy. I guess her skirts are long enough.

Latvia is very close to Germany. It's strange thinking about someone in your own family being so close to all that trouble. But Uncle Izzy didn't say a single word about Hitler or Nazis in his letter, so I guess I shouldn't worry.

January 20

At St. Chris today, I overheard one of the ladies who work there talking about Hitler with one of the other ladies. It was Miss McTavish, the thin one with the curly blond hair. Anyway, Miss McTavish told the other lady that *The Star* says the Nazis are out of fashion in Germany now. Thank goodness. I can stop worrying about Uncle Izzy and my new aunt. I can't wait to tell Benny.

January 23

It's so exciting! Miss McTavish told me that there's going to be a Spring Festival this year, and she asked me if I'd like to be in it! She said she wants to find five girls to do a dance for spring to some music called "The Waltz of the Flowers" by a composer named Tchaikovsky. His name sounds Jewish to me. I wonder if he is. Anyway, Miss McTavish played a record of the music for me, and it was glorious. You could just see the flowers dancing. I couldn't help humming along.

I said I'd do it! Maybe I can't be an opera singer, but I can be a ballet dancer, which is even better. That'll show that crazy Miss Tedde.

The only problem is, I don't have any dancing slippers, and Miss McTavish says I can practise without them but I can't be in the festival if I don't have them, because of course dancers can't dance on stage without dancing slippers. She said that maybe she could get some for me if I didn't have my own, but of course I can't let her. Pa would kill me. I told her I would get some, but I don't know how I ever will.

I told Benny about Hitler being out of fashion and he said the reporters in *The Star* are just a bunch of *meshuggeneh goyim* who don't know what they're talking about. He's such a know-it-all. That's not what he said when *The Star* had news he wanted to hear.

January 24

Pa had a letter from his cousin Yankl today. It took him a while, but he made it to Montreal okay. There's no work for him in the deli, but he says not to worry. He's going to look for a job in Montreal for a while, but he doesn't want to go on relief, so if nothing turns up maybe he'll take the train back to Saskatchewan — or even all the way to Vancouver. Now he knows how to do it, he thinks that riding the rails isn't so dangerous after all.

I hope he'll be okay.

January 26

We had our first practice for the spring festival. Rivka is in it, too, and some other girls I don't know, but they seem nice for girls who are only in Senior Three.

Dancing is harder than it looks. Miss McTavish says I'll find it easier once I get my dancing slippers. The festival isn't until March. I still have almost two months to get the slippers. Maybe a miracle will happen. You never know.

Of course Rivka has her slippers already. I don't care, I'd rather have lots of sisters to talk to than dancing slippers.

January 30

I finished reading *Phronsie Pepper*. It's my fourth book about the Peppers, and they're still okay, but I think I'm getting a little tired of them. It was wonderful when they were poor and happy and baking cakes in the Little Brown House, but now they're even happier and everyone they ever meet loves them all to death, especially Phronsie because of her beautiful blond hair, and they are so rich now that it's ridiculous. They live in a fancy mansion and spend all their time going to fancy parties and talking about how wonderful it was when they were poor in the Little Brown House. I wish I was rich and had a mansion and could spend all my time talking about how wonderful it was when we used to be poor in 29 Leonard Avenue.

Right now it doesn't feel very wonderful. We haven't had a chicken for Shabbes for weeks, and there are hardly any of the potatoes left that Pa bought last fall, and I don't know what will happen when they're gone because potatoes are so expensive to buy now in the middle of winter, even wholesale at the Terminal. I don't see how I'm ever going to be able to pay back Mrs. Koslov for that movie, let alone get dancing slippers. Pa hardly ever even gets the furnace going. It's very depressing.

February 1

Today on the radio I heard that song they play all the time — the sad one about the man who was a millionaire but then he lost all his money because of the Depression. Anyway, I was humming along when I started to think about the words:

Once I built a railroad, now it's done.

Brother, can you spare a dime?

It's very sad. But golly, a dime is a lot of money. In our family, these days there's not even a nickel to spare. Not even a penny. The man in the song has a lot of nerve asking for a whole dime.

February 2

Benny came around yesterday with a copy of the *Yiddishe* newspaper, the *Zhurnal,* that he got from one of the men in the belt factory. It says that the Nazi man, Hitler, has become the chancellor in Germany! The chancellor is the boss of the whole country! Hitler sure wasn't out of fashion for very long.

The *Zhurnal* says that the Nazis will just eat up all the Jews. It must be awful for them there, just awful.

Benny told me it could happen here, too, if we don't watch out — right here in Canada. I told him he was *meshugge,* like I always do when he talks about Germany, but I guess I said it once too often, because this time he got really mad at me. Really, really mad. He called me a spoiled little baby and then I called him a know-it-all and a smart alec and then he just gave me a look and stomped off and went home. I don't care. Who needs him anyway?

February 5

I've been thinking about it, and I've decided that Benny is *meshugge,* completely *meshugge.* It can't really be that bad in Germany, can it? And it certainly couldn't ever happen here in Canada, not ever. Not in a million years. Uncle Izzy sure wasn't worried about it in his letter, and he lives much closer to Germany than we do. I'm going to just forget about it and think about more pleasant things. I'm going to be glad no matter what, like Pollyanna in that wonderful book I read last year. It was truly inspiring.

One pleasant thing is that Syd Schein came around and dragged Sophie off to a meeting of the Jewish Juniors at Diana Sweets. Sophie didn't want to go, but Syd made her. I wouldn't want to go either — who wants to hear a bunch of old ladies making speeches? But it must be the first time Sophie's gone anywhere but work or shopping with Ma in the market since she stopped seeing that freckly Steven. Maybe now she'll stop being such a mope all the time. Sure, I feel sorry for her. But if you ask me, it's about time she got over it. Good for Syd.

February 8

I haven't seen Benny, not once. I think he's still mad at me, and I don't care, because I'm still mad at him. I'm sure Benny's overreacting about Hitler. Positive.

I have to stop writing now. Molly wants me to help her brush her hair. And anyway, I don't have anything worth writing about.

February 9

Ma was over visiting Auntie Esther today, and Auntie Esther told her that Benny stopped working at the belt factory because he got a new job. Auntie Esther doesn't know what the job is, but she says it must be a good one because Benny has been giving her lots of grocery money and he's such a good son.

I wonder what the job is. I know Benny hated the belt factory, but he was making pretty good money there — at least as much as my sisters make, which isn't much, I guess, but it's something. Anyway, what kind of job could Benny get that pays more? Not that I really care, of course, because Benny means nothing to me. Less than nothing. In fact, his name will never appear in my diary ever again. He's out of my life forever, and that makes me really, really glad.

I am very bored.

February 13

It's much more peaceful when that person whose name I refuse to mention ever again isn't around. I've just been going to school and doing homework and cleaning house and looking after Molly and Hindl. School is okay, I guess. We just seem to do the same arithmetic problems and the same spelling exercises and the same geography lessons all the time. I am so tired of the names of the capitals of the nine provinces. Who cares where Fredericton is? The only interesting thing I've done is go to practise "The Waltz of the Flowers." We're getting to be very good — even me, and I know I'll be ever so much better if I ever get dancing slippers.

February 15

I wish I knew what ~~B~~ that person's new job is. I can't help it. I can't stop thinking about it. The track is closed now, so he can't be a table, can he? I really, really hope he isn't doing something illegal again. Not because of him, of course. Because of Auntie Esther. Because of the family.

I know what the job is, and I am so, so worried about ~~B~~ that person BENNY. There. I wrote it, and I'm going to write it again. BENNY BENNY BENNY. I'm so worried about Benny that I just can't be mad at him anymore.

He came over last night just as if nothing had ever happened and asked me if I'd like to go to Altman's and get a soda because he was buying because he had lots and lots of money because of his new job. I tried to stay mad at him, but I just couldn't resist asking him where the money came from.

He said he wouldn't tell me unless I promised not to tell anybody else. He even got me to cross my heart and hope to die. Pa caught me doing that once and told me never to do it again because it's not a Jewish thing to do. But I did it anyway when Benny asked, because I was dying to know.

Benny works for a bootlegger!

Before Benny told me, I didn't even know what a bootlegger is. It's someone who makes booze in their own house. The bootlegger makes the booze and sells it to other people — and it's illegal, just like I thought it would be.

If you ask me, liquor is bad enough even when it's the legal kind. It makes people act crazy. Like my

Uncle Max, for instance. I told that to Benny, too. He agreed, but he said before I started saying bad things about bootleggers I should remember my pa is one, too.

That made me so furious I almost stopped talking to Benny all over again. I would have if I wasn't so worried about him.

My pa is not a bootlegger. My pa never did a bad or illegal thing in his entire life — except for driving into that limousine, and that wasn't his fault, no matter what the judge said.

Oh sure, Pa makes wine. Gosh, I'm leaning against the wine barrel right now while I'm writing, aren't I? And Ma and Pa both drink a glass on Shabbes, and they even let the rest of us have a little sip each at the *seder* on Pesach. It tastes really horrible, but you have to drink it if you want to be a good Jew.

But that's why Pa makes it, because we need it for praying every Friday. The kind of booze the bootlegger makes isn't wine and it has nothing to do with praying. It just gets people drunk. What is Benny thinking of?

Benny's job is to be a lookout. The bootlegger lives in a house up the lane behind Baldwin, close to Spadina on the other side of the market. Benny says the lady who sells the booze calls it rye whiskey, but it's really made out of tea and brown sugar and things like that, and she charges them 25¢ to buy just one glass! You could buy a whole pound of meat for that much money! Anyway, Benny is just supposed to stand there at the beginning of the lane and watch out for the police. If a policeman comes, he's supposed to run up the lane and knock on the door three times, and then the bootlegger knows she has to get rid of any customers she has in there and hide everything before the policeman comes.

So far, Benny says, there haven't been any policemen. He says he's making good money for doing nothing at all, which is much better than working in the belt factory or slaving away at Uncle Bertzik's for peanuts like my sisters do. But what if a policeman does come and he arrests Benny and puts him in jail? I tried to talk Benny into quitting but he just laughed at me. What can he be thinking of? Maybe all those hits his father gives him have scrambled his brains. I am so worried about him.

I really shouldn't be. He didn't even apologize for walking out like that. He didn't even seem to realize I was mad at him about it or about Hitler. And the real reason he came around was because he needs me. His band is playing for an afternoon tea at another Church of England church, on Manning Avenue about five blocks from here, and he wants me to help with the drums again. He begged and begged until I said I would. I agreed to do it because I'm so worried about him.

February 19

The Church of England people just sat around drinking tea. None of them danced or anything, not even once. I hummed along to everything. It felt good, and I decided I don't care about Miss Tedde. What does she know anyway? I'll sing if I feel like it, in as high a voice as I want. The band sounded very good, and Benny was still looking pretty elegant even though he had some stains on the tuxedo from carrying drums and things. It's a pity it's a white one.

After the dance, some Church of England boys came up and started talking to the band, and Harvey Tischler ended up challenging them to a hockey game, the *Yids* against the *goyim*. I couldn't play, of course. What if my hat fell off and they found out I was a girl? And anyway, who wants to go out and get bumped around by a bunch of rough boys? Not me. I hate sports. And besides, I don't know how to play. I was going to just leave and go home by myself, but I couldn't, because then they'd be stuck with all the drums. So I stayed and watched. Benny told the *goy-*

ishe boys that I was recovering from a serious illness and wasn't allowed. Harvey Tischler whispered to me that it was the serious illness of being a girl. Ho ho. Very funny.

When we got outside, Harvey took some horse-balls out of his pockets — he actually had three of them in there! Isn't that disgusting? Then he put me in charge of them, and that was even more disgusting. I had to pick one up and throw it out whenever the one they were using fell apart. Now my mittens smell almost as bad as Harvey's do. Why can't I just enjoy being a girl and play with dolls and learn how to sew properly? Rivka would never pick up a horse-ball, that's for sure.

Still, the game was exciting. We won, too, 10–8. Benny scored three times.

After the game, I brought Benny back to have supper. At least it kept him away from the bootleg-ger for a few hours. You could tell Ma was angry about it, but she sent me down here to the cellar to get another potato to put in the pot for him anyway. There are hardly any left.

February 23

A terrible, terrible thing happened. I found Benny on the front porch this morning, shivering and shaking and nearly freezing to death — the radio said it was just 39° this morning. Benny had blood on his face and his scarf, and he looked awful. I wanted to get Ma or Pa, but he said no, he'd just go away if I tried to. So I snuck him down the outside stairs into the cellar. I didn't know what else to do. He actually fell sound asleep leaning against the coal bin before I got back with my winter blanket and a big hunk of bread I managed to get from the kitchen. Lucky nobody saw me. Then I had to throw the blanket over Benny and rush off to school. I didn't want to leave him alone, because what if someone came down and found him? Ma would be scared out of her wits, and Pa would probably think he was a hobo or something and clop him over the head with an orange crate before he even looked to see who it was. But I didn't have a choice. I didn't find out what happened to Benny until I rushed home at lunchtime.

It turns out that Benny was doing his lookout job for the bootlegger, and guess who showed up there to buy a drink? Uncle Max, of course. Benny should have realized his pa would be a customer.

On his way to the bootlegger's, Uncle Max saw Benny standing there at the beginning of the lane and told him to stop loitering in the streets like a no-good bum and go home — so Benny had to pretend to leave while his pa went up the lane. But then, after Uncle Max went into the house, Benny came back to do his lookout job — which was when Uncle Max suddenly rushed out of the house and grabbed Benny and gave him a big hit, right there on the street. Benny has a huge bruise on his cheek, and he's really mad at his pa. He says that's why he didn't go home all night and stayed on our porch. But really, I think he's scared of Uncle Max. If it was me, I'd sure be scared. I'm so lucky to have Pa. He may be strict, but he would never hit us.

What happened was, the bootlegger lady somehow knew that Uncle Max was Benny's father and so she told him what a good job Benny was doing for her. She didn't know that Uncle Max didn't know that Benny was working there. It made Uncle Max furious — not because bootlegging is a bad thing, but because Benny was keeping the job a secret and keeping all the money for himself. Uncle Max didn't know Benny was giving most of the money to his ma, and of course Benny didn't tell him, or else Uncle Max would have just made Auntie Esther give it to him.

Benny left our place as soon as he finished telling me what happened. He said he didn't want to get me into trouble for hiding him. I wish he hadn't gone. I don't know where he is now, and it really

scares me. I hope he isn't freezing to death somewhere.

February 24

I have snuck down to the cellar to write this
because I am so, so relieved. Benny is okay! He went
and told his brother Al about what happened, and Al
and his wife Rita said Benny could sleep on the
chesterfield in their apartment until things cooled
down between him and Uncle Max. Benny says
they're never going to cool down because he's never
going to have anything to do with his pa ever again.
I feel so sorry for him.

Ma is calling everyone to watch her light the
Shabbes candles. I have to go.

February 27

I took *Phronsie Pepper* back to the big library and
I decided I'm not reading any more about the
Peppers, even though there are still at least seven
more books. I am sick to death of them and their
stupid Little Brown House. Nothing bad ever happens to them. It just isn't real. They never get into
fights with their relatives and end up with bloody
faces. They never ride the rails or work for bootleggers. And they never remember how hungry they

must have been when they were poor. I can't forget it. I'm sick and tired of potatoes. And this week, Ma had to borrow some money from Uncle Bertzik again. Pa knew, but this time he didn't say anything, because what choice do we have?

Well, at least there's one good thing — Benny is back at the belt factory. It seems Al wouldn't let him stay at his place if he kept on working for the bootlegger. The belt factory may be a little dangerous, but at least it isn't illegal.

March 3

On the way to school today, I had to walk out onto the road because the sidewalk just down the street was covered with furniture. It was the Letinskys' furniture — they live at number 45. Or, I guess, they *used to* live there. They must have got kicked out by the landlord because they couldn't pay the rent. I guess the landlord had someone else who wanted the house, or else he'd probably have let them stay. Ma told me she heard Mr. Letinsky couldn't find any work, and the rest of their family are too poor to help them.

Mrs. Letinsky was sitting on an ugly green chesterfield with holes in the arms, holding onto her baby and looking very sad. I guess she was guarding the furniture against thieves until Mr. Letinsky could find someone to lend him a truck and figure out where to take their stuff. I'm sure Pa would have let them use his truck if it was running, but of course it's not summer yet and it still has the tires off. I couldn't think of anything to say to her, so I just pretended I didn't see her and walked by. But I've been thinking about the Letinskys all day. It's so sad. What will they do now?

March 5

Another disaster. I must be the most clumsy, most useless person on the face of the entire planet. I feel just awful.

It happened when I was practising my steps for "The Waltz of the Flowers" down in the cellar this morning. I went there because of course it's the only place I can go where no one can see me. If I stayed upstairs, Gert would just make stupid jokes and laugh at me and Molly and Hindl would start imitating me and getting in the way. Anyway, I was whirling around with my arms way out like they're supposed to be and one of my hands bumped into one of the big jugs of wine Pa made last fall and it fell over and all the wine spilled out onto the ground.

Ma and Pa are furious. Now they'll have hardly

any wine for Shabbes until next fall when the grapes are ripe and Pa can make some more. I feel so guilty.

And now I can't possibly ever ask them about getting the dancing slippers. I wish I could just roll over and die right now.

March 6

Ma heard from Mrs. Goldstein that the Letinskys had to sell all their furniture to a second-hand store and move in with Mrs. Letinsky's brother in a small apartment on Bathurst Street. There's just one bedroom, and there are eight of them living there now! We are so lucky to have a whole house. I promise I won't ever complain about having to share a room with Gert, never ever again.

I still feel bad about not talking to Mrs. Letinsky last Friday. After all, they've been our neighbours for years. And I can't stop thinking of what it must feel like to get kicked out of your own house. But she was probably too sad to even notice me.

Let's see, what else happened? Oh yes, Benny is still going on and on about politics. To begin with, that Hitler and his Nazi party won an election in Germany, which is bad enough. But also, Benny has been spending a lot of time with some men in the factory who want to start a union. Benny wants one, too. He says the bosses are mean to the workers and hardly pay them anything. He told his ma, and his ma told his pa, and his pa is happy about it and he and Benny are actually getting along for a change. I'm glad they are, I guess, but I wish it wasn't because Benny is turning into one of those godless communists who want to cause trouble for everybody, like Pa is always saying. At least he isn't getting hit.

Benny was also all excited about some law he read about in the *Zhurnal* that they're trying to get the government of Ontario to pass. It's to stop people from picking on Jews, but Benny also says there's no chance it will happen. He went on and on about all the places that are restricted to Jews. He says that Jews can't live anywhere in Toronto except right around here where we live, and now that some Jews are starting to move in up north past our neighbourhood, around Christie Pits park, the *goyim* are furious about it and who knows what might happen? The *goyim* say they want to keep Canada British, but Benny says that just means no Jews allowed, and that it's almost as bad here as it is in Germany.

I hate it when he talks like that. It scares me. But I guess I can put up with it, because I have to admit it, things are more interesting when he's around.

March 7

I was sitting down in the cellar after school feeling sorry for myself when Dora came down to get some beets to cook for supper. There are still a few left. They're kind of limp but you can still eat them. Dora asked me what was the matter and she looked so worried about me that I couldn't help myself. I told her all about the spring festival and dancing "The Waltz of the Flowers" and how I wasn't going to be able to be in the concert because I wouldn't have any dancing slippers. Dora gave me a big hug and told me not to give up so easily. It made me feel much better. I'll try not to give up, even though I know I should. Maybe a miracle will happen. You never know.

March 8

I'm beginning to think that Benny may be right. I met him on the street yesterday on the way back from the big library. He was carrying boxes of buckles back to the factory from a buckle wholesaler on Spadina. We were walking down College Street, and we noticed there was a policeman walking behind us. Benny said we should speed up. I didn't see why we should, but he started walking faster so I had to, too. Then the policeman came right up and kicked me in the behind and said, "Move over, you no-good little kike. Do you think you own the sidewalk?" Those are his exact words. I will remember them forever. Then he just gave us a dirty look and went on down the street.

Benny was furious. I had to hold onto his coat to stop him from running after the policeman and yelling at him and getting thrown into jail or something.

I wasn't angry, just humiliated. I told Benny I was all right, but I couldn't wait to come home and come down to the cellar where I could cry in peace. I am never going to tell anyone else about it, either. If anyone knew, I would die.

Kike is an awful word. How could a policeman do that to me? So what if he didn't know I'm a girl? I'm a British citizen, aren't I?

And how did he know I was Jewish? Do I look Jewish? I guess I do. And I'm proud of it, too. I'm proud to be a kike, even if it's an awful, nasty thing for someone to call you.

But maybe Pa doesn't know everything. Maybe just sticking to your own kind isn't enough.

March 9

Today in school we were supposed to be working on our arithmetic problems but I got distracted and started thinking about not sticking to your own kind, because of course we always do. I mean, I talk to Rivka and some of the other Jewish girls all the time, but none of us ever talk to any of the *goyishe* girls. And of course they never talk to us, they just look down their noses at us when they pass by like they were smelling a bad smell or something. I guess we do the same to them, too, but still. Some of those girls have been in my class right through school all the way from Junior One, and I know their names from the roll call and what colour their hair is and what kinds of dresses they wear, but that's all I know about them. I know more about the Jewish boys, for heavens' sake, and of course we hardly ever talk to any of them, either.

Maybe it would be interesting to know some of the *goyishe* girls, even just a little. The one I'd really like to know is Myoshi Ukeda. I know she lives just a block away, over on Bellevue, because I see her walking there on the way home from school. And she looks so strange and interesting and exotic, like Madame Butterfly in the opera in the book Sophie got from the library about operas. I wonder what it's like in her house and what kind of food they eat.

She's the only Japanese girl in the whole neighbourhood. I don't think she even has any sisters or brothers. She always plays by herself and walks home by herself. She must be so lonely.

But of course I can't just go up to her and start talking. What would she think? What would Rivka or the other girls think? And I could never talk to Myrtle MacDonald, even if we like the same things, because who knows, a *goyishe* girl like her might come from a family who thinks Jews should all be rounded up and sent back to the old country. She might think so herself. I could never do it. I guess I don't even really want to.

But still, I sort of wish I did.

If I did and that horrible policeman saw us, he'd have a conniption fit.

March 14

According to Benny, the *Zhurnal* agrees with him that it's going to be really bad for the Jews in Germany now that horrible Hitler person has won the election there, and also bad for us here. He got me really worried, so I decided to go ask Sophie about it. Sophie is so smart, and she reads lots of books and magazines, and she always thinks she knows everything. I would have asked her before, but she was so mopey all the time and you could never get a word out of her except "Go away and leave me alone." I'm so glad she's starting to be herself again, even if she is always telling me to stand up straighter and making sure I have my homework done so I can get good grades and be the first one in the family to finish high school and maybe even go to college. It's just like it used to be. Oh well.

Anyway, Sophie told me Benny was all wrong and I shouldn't listen to him. She says she heard people on the radio saying that Hitler in Germany will be just like Mussolini in Italy and he's organized and efficient and getting the trains to run on time and more countries should have leaders like him. She says Hitler says bad things about Jews, but so do the *goyim* here and nothing really bad ever happens. It's all just talk.

I hope she's right. But if she is, why is the *Zhurnal* writing all those scary things that Benny keeps telling me about?

March 16

It was still chilly out today. Poor Molly lost a mitten in the backyard and I had to help her find it and it took forever and I nearly froze. I wish spring would come.

We had a spelling bee after supper in the kitchen yesterday. We haven't had one for ages and ages — not since last year before Steven. Sophie said she was having it because me being interested in Hitler was a good sign. She says I need to learn everything I can and if I do, I will go far and make the family and maybe even the whole Jewish community proud and show *anti-semits* like Hitler how smart we all are. So she made me and Gert spell words for her. Gert lost, of course. She couldn't even spell *minimal* — she put two *n*s in it. Really! How could she? But I guess if I were her and I knew Sophie was just having the spelling bee for me then I wouldn't try either. Still, I wish Dora had been there and not Gert, because my arm is so sore from all the pinches Gert gave me after. Gert would be so happy if she knew I got two wrong on a spelling test at school yesterday. I had *cooly* instead of *coolly* and *wierd* instead of *weird*. I'll never tell her, that's for sure. And anyway, it was an especially hard test, and Myrtle MacDonald had two wrong, too, the same two as me.

March 19

I have dancing slippers! And it's all because of Dora. Who needs Polly Pepper when I already have Dora! Wonderful, wonderful Dora, the best sister ever!

Yesterday morning, Dora was very mysterious.

She waited until Gert was in the bathroom and then she came down to my room and invited me to go out for a walk. But then instead of walking, she took me on the streetcar and we ended up downtown at Eaton's Annex, and she said that if we could find some we could afford, she was going to buy me dancing slippers!

We were in luck! They had a whole table of dancing slippers on sale for 25¢, and we found a pair that fit me almost perfectly. They're seconds, of course, but there's just a small flaw in one of the seams that Ma can fix. They are perfectly lovely.

Before we bought the slippers, Dora made me promise not to tell Ma and Pa where they came from, and I said I'd say that Miss Douglas bought them for everyone in the concert. Dora almost always gives every cent she makes to Ma and Pa, and they were upset with her when she gave them less money this week than usual. She said it was because she made mistakes cutting fabric and had her pay docked, and Pa got mad and told her to try to be more careful. She was just being nice to me. If Pa only knew, he'd feel so rotten.

After we bought the slippers, we went through the tunnel between the Annex and the main store to get to the streetcar stop. There's a place down there that sells ice-cream waffles. They make the waffles right there and they smell so, so good — almost like the Ex. I couldn't help but mention to Dora how good they smelled, and Dora agreed — and she said there was still a little left because the slippers were so cheap, so she went up to the man and bought a waffle for each of us! They were scrumptious! I know I should feel guilty about eating them when there's so little food for us all. But I don't. Yesterday was the best day ever.

I guess I do feel just a bit guilty. Today for lunch I think I'm going to give Hindl my share of the cottage cheese and just have a glass of water.

March 23

I am in heaven!! The spring festival was last night, and it was truly wonderful. Being on stage is so glamorous. The dancing dresses that Miss McTavish and the other St. Chris ladies made were all filmy and sparkly and looked like giant daffodils, and you could hardly notice the flaw in my slippers at all. Miss McTavish said we all danced divinely, and I think we did, too.

Ma and Pa weren't there, of course. They never come to St. Chris. Sometimes I wonder why they let us all go when they won't go themselves, but Ma just says we know who we are. Don't she and Pa know who they are? Of course they do. Last year, I tried to get Ma to go and take English lessons there, like lots of Jewish men and women do. But she refused. She said everyone she knows speaks Yiddish, so what was the point? I bet she could learn English real fast if she wanted to. Pa, too — he can speak some English, of course, but he could learn more. Then they could talk to people who come to the door instead of depending on Sophie and me. But they'd rather just stay home.

Sophie was out at a meeting with Syd again, so Dora and Gert were the only ones who came. Dora said it was wonderful and worth every penny she spent on the slippers, and of course I thanked her again and again and again. Gert sat at the back and spent the whole time not paying any attention and giggling with some boys from the St. Chris wood-working club. And afterwards, all she did was make a nasty comment about my arms, just like she always does.

March 25

Benny came over with his ma for tea. He brought the front page from Thursday's *Star* with him, with a huge headline at the top saying *Jews Flee in Terror from Nazi Torture*. There was a story about Jews being beaten and forced to drink castor oil to make them sick and another one about a Jewish man who was dragged out of his bed by Nazis and taken to a lonely spot in the woods and shot. I couldn't tell if Benny was more upset about it happening or more happy because he was right about Hitler all along. As for me, it just makes me sick. It's very frightening. I don't even want to think about it. But I can't stop.

March 28

This morning in school one of the *goyishe* girls, Angelina del Nardi, fainted right in the middle of History. Miss Douglas was talking about all the countries in the British Empire and Angelina just keeled over and fell on the floor. Afterwards, she told Miss Douglas it was probably because she was hungry, because it was her turn to miss breakfast this morning. She said someone in her family always has to miss it because there isn't enough for them all. Miss Douglas looked angry, but she gave Angelina half the sandwich she brought for herself for lunch.

I feel so sorry for Angelina. We may not have much, but at least there's always a little bit for everybody.

I wonder if the Depression is ever going to end.

April 3

I'm so worried about Gert. She's been sneaking out at night to meet a boy, and she says she'll kill me if I say anything about it to anybody and I know she probably would, too, because she's so mean.

It's a boy named Chaim, and she met him at the spring concert. Benny knows Chaim from Altman's and he says he's a waste of space. He only went to woodworking at St. Chris so he could sneak out some of the tools they have there and sell them to buy cigarettes.

Gert's way too young to be interested in boys. Especially a *gonif* like that Chaim.

April 7

I'm glad spring is here and the days are longer. It means I can write something on Friday after school and before Shabbes begins.

I have a lot to write, because I've been so worried about Gert that I forgot to put down all the things Benny has been telling me about. Or maybe I just didn't want to. It's all so horrible. That monster Hitler has been doing all the things in Germany that Benny said he would. Benny read in the *Zhurnal* that Hitler has thrown out all the Jewish doctors and lawyers and he's making kosher meat illegal and he says he wants the whole country of Germany to be cleansed of Jews. Cleansed — that's what he said, like we're lice or something. On April Fool's Day they had a boycott against Jewish stores, and they weren't fooling. Benny says lots of Jewish people are trying to get out of Germany. If I were them I'd be trying to get out, too. I'm so worried about them, and I'm so glad we're here.

Benny says we should be doing something about it. Lots of people are. He says there was a big rally in New York at Madison Square Garden and they filled it up with thousands and thousands of people inside and there were even more outside. And there was even a rally right here in Toronto at Massey Hall, and Benny went to it! He heard all kinds of people make speeches about how bad Hitler is. He says there were lots of *goyishe* people there, not just Jews. Doesn't that mean that things are better here?

Benny says, no, it doesn't, because there are lots of people right here in Toronto who are on Hitler's side. He says he went to a boxing match last week between a Jewish boxer and a German one. It was in a club above a store on Spadina, and the crowd was half Jews and half Germans and there was nearly a riot. I wish Benny wouldn't go to all those danger- ous places. And I'm certainly not going to let him talk me into going with him ever, ever again. Anyway, it'll soon be too warm to wear that stupid reefer coat, thank goodness, and so I can't pretend to be a boy anymore. I just wish he wouldn't go either.

It's almost dark. Time for Shabbes.

April 12

It's Pesach now, and Ma has been busy cleaning the whole house from top to bottom and I've been helping whenever I can. I wish I didn't have so much homework. Miss Douglas gets so upset when we take time off school for Jewish holidays that she gives us all sorts of extra work. It's totally unfair.

The first *seder* was last night. We didn't have a chicken or anything fancy, and to begin with, it hardly even felt like Pesach. But Ma said even if we couldn't afford fancy food we could still celebrate, and we did. Ma bought a little bit of meat to make stew from, and the butcher threw in some bones. He said it was for the dog and Ma didn't tell him we don't have a dog, she just said thank you and took the bones. The stew was mostly potatoes but it was delicious, and it felt so good to have everyone there all together, especially when I know all the bad things that are happening to other people like the Jews in Germany and poor Angelina del Nardi. I guess we're lucky. This year, I didn't ask the questions because Molly can read a little now and she got to do it for the first time.

Molly turned beet red and looked really, really nervous. She stumbled a few times, but not much. She may not be the smartest one, but she tries hard, and she has a good heart.

Molly asked the questions in English, the way I always did. Pa said she did a good job, but I could tell he was a little unhappy. Poor Pa. He always wanted a son to carry on his name, and he never got one.

April 21

Pa was laid off from Christie's yesterday. Now what will we do for money? Ma wants to ask Uncle Bertzik to give Pa a job at the factory, but Pa won't let her. He says he'll go on relief before he ever takes a job from Ma's brother. I know what that means — it means he'll never do it. Pa thinks that only cowards and weaklings go on relief. And besides, the relief people come and inspect the house and look under the beds and open all the cupboards and make sure you're not hiding anything before they give you even a penny. I know because Benny's ma had to have it last year when she was sick, and the lady who came was really nasty to her and even looked in her underwear drawer. Benny says he nearly hit her.

But Pa being out of work isn't the worst thing. The worst thing is, I went into the parlour last night to listen to the radio and Gert was there on the sofa in the dark with Chaim. They were smooching! I nearly died. They were practically sitting on top of each other. It was very, very embarrassing. Gert turned bright red and Chaim told me he'd give me a nickel if I went away. I didn't know what to do so I just took it and went.

I was so mad at Gert that I went right to the back door and I threw the nickel into the backyard.

I should tell Ma. Or maybe I shouldn't. She has so many things to worry about now. And Gert would be so mad if I told. It really isn't my business. Is it? I don't know what to do.

April 23

I couldn't stop thinking about that nickel Chaim gave me. I mean, a nickel is a nickel. Finally, I snuck out into the yard this morning when no one was watching and I found it again, hidden in the grass. I should give it to Ma except she'll ask where I got it and then I'll have to tell her about Gert. I don't want to tell her. Why does everything have to happen to me?

April 26

Harvey Tischler isn't in Benny's band anymore, and Benny says it's all my fault. All I did was refuse to go with them last Saturday when they played in a dance hall somewhere in the west end. I told Benny I had other things to do, but really, I just didn't feel like it. Benny always acts like he's my boss or something, and I don't like it. I guess I should have gone — I had to spend the whole afternoon playing paper dolls with Molly and Hindl, and guess what? Molly wanted my paper doll to be the maid and she gave me such a sweet smile that I just couldn't say no, even though I wanted to. Dolly Dingle is supposed to be a little girl, not a maid. Sometimes life makes me want to just scream.

Anyway, Benny says the only way the band could get to the dance hall was by getting off the streetcar and then taking a rowboat across a stream. Because I wasn't there, Harvey had to go back across the stream three times to carry all his equipment — the others helped him with it on the streetcar, but they refused to do the stream. Anyway, Harvey got tired from the rowing and it made him so mad he quit. Poor little baby. Harvey is such a *kvetcher*. If you ask me, the band is better off without him. Now that spring is here and everything is beginning to thaw, his clothes must stink to high heaven. Anyway, now it's just the sax and the fiddle and Benny in his dirty white suit. And I don't care what Benny says, it's *not* my fault.

Gert is still sneaking out all the time. She told me if I tell Ma and Pa she will make my life miserable forever. I can't imagine how she can be any meaner to me than she is already, but I bet she could if she tried.

I still have that nickel, and I still haven't told Ma.

May 2

Pa finally got a job. He's working in the St. Lawrence Market, stacking empty crates. One of the men from the Fruit Terminal has a brother who knows the man who gave Pa the job. Pa says it isn't much, but it's a job, and he's lucky to have one, because there are so many people out of work.

It's true. A lot of them don't even have a house to live in anymore — just like Pa's cousin Yankl. We still haven't heard anything more from him. I wonder how he is, and where he is. I started thinking about him because yesterday morning when I took Hindl for a swing before school, there was a man sleeping on the bench in the park. They seem to be there all the time now. This one was snoring very loudly and his clothes were wrinkled and filthy like Yankl's were, and he smelled almost as bad as Harvey Tischler. I felt really sorry for him.

We're so lucky, we really are. Sophie and Dora and Gert are sewing, and now Pa has a job, too. So we'll be okay even if we are in the middle of a Depression. But I do worry a lot about Yankl.

May 4

I was in the library at St. Chris and I noticed they had a book called *Robinson Crusoe* and I suddenly remembered that movie last winter with Douglas Fairbanks and the money Mrs. Koslov gave me to get in. And then I thought about that nickel of Chaim's. I still haven't given it to Ma, even though I know I should, and I hate the thought of it sitting there tied up in a sock at the bottom of my dresser drawer reminding me of what a coward I am. So I've decided I'm going to give the nickel to Mrs. Koslov.

May 5

Mrs. Koslov said she'd totally forgotten about the movie and thanked me for the nickel and told me to forget about the other 5¢ and told me what a good girl I am for remembering. If only she knew. I still haven't told Ma about Chaim. I just can't.

The most ridiculous thing happened. Well, Dora doesn't think it was at all funny. Poor Dora, I do feel sorry for her, I really do. But whenever I think of it I can't help laughing. I am such a terrible, terrible person, I really am.

Mr. Roitenberg came around yesterday to collect the rent, and of course Ma said she was a little short, because of course she almost always is. Usually, Mr. Roitenberg just makes a sour face like he's burping and gives her a few more days. But not yesterday. Yesterday, he told Ma he had a solution to the problem.

You'll never guess what it was! He wanted to marry Dora! He said if he did he'd hardly charge any rent at all to his in-laws!

Ma didn't even have to think about it for a minute. She just told him that Dora was much too young.

Maybe she is, but if you ask me, the real problem is that Mr. Roitenberg is much too old. He must be at least a hundred and fifty and he has a big grey beard and wrinkles and his suit always smells bad. Just thinking about my dear darling Dora and that disgusting old man standing under the *chuppah* together to get married makes me laugh. Dora deserves better than that, even if Mr. Roitenberg does own four houses.

The worst part is, Ma had to come up with the missing rent money right there on the spot, and now there's no money for food for the rest of the week. We'll just have to make do with what we've got. I am so sick of oatmeal.

May 11

We're starting a new sewing project in Domestic Science. It's a sundress. We're going to cut out the pieces this week, and it should be all finished by the time school stops. I wish I could make a dress with sleeves instead, but there probably won't be enough material and the teacher wouldn't let me anyway because sleeves are so hard to do.

It was really warm today. Soon it'll be warm enough to wear a sundress, and I'll have one to wear!

May 13

Benny's pa is in big trouble. He's working for the furriers' union now, and on Thursday he went into a factory in the Tower Building on Spadina to hand out pamphlets about a walkout to the women working there making up coats. The supervisor got mad at him and told him to get out before he called the police. Uncle Max swore at him and they started to shout at each other and Uncle Max got so mad he ended up picking up a big pair of scissors and stabbing the supervisor right in the back! Can you imagine! They had to take the supervisor to a doctor, and the doctor called the police. Benny says the supervisor might press charges if he doesn't get better. Benny doesn't think he will, because his pa says the supervisor came from the old country not so long ago and he's not a citizen yet. He only got to be a supervisor because his brother owns the factory and if he makes any trouble they might send him back. Benny says it doesn't get into the papers or anything, but his friends at the belt factory know about all sorts of men who got sent back to Europe for doing nothing at all. The *goyim* do it so they can keep the jobs for their own kind.

Benny says his pa says it'll be different when the socialists take over. What I'd like to know is, since when did Benny start listening to his pa? He gets mad at Uncle Max for hitting him and everything, he refuses to live in the same house with him and sleeps on a hard old sofa in his brother Al's place, but he still believes everything his pa says. I wish he wouldn't. My pa is right — socialists like uncle Max are just troublemakers and they make the *goyim* mad and make it bad for the rest of us. The last thing we need is more trouble.

May 21

Like Ma always says, if it isn't one thing it's another. Now that it's warm enough, Pa doesn't have to smoke in the cellar anymore. He can go outside. Last night he says he couldn't sleep so he went out to the front porch to have a cigarette, and guess what? He caught Gert trying to sneak in! She said she was just out with a girlfriend, but Pa saw that *trombenik* Chaim running off down the sidewalk.

Pa was so mad he yelled at Gert right out there on the porch. I didn't hear anything because I was sound asleep upstairs, but I bet all the neighbours heard. Pa told Gert she could never see Chaim ever again — just like he told Sophie about Steven. After Gert came up to our room she woke me up and told me and she cried and cried and cried. I gave her a big hug to make her feel better, and I think it did. But really and truly, I'm glad it happened. I'll never have to talk to that no-goodnik Chaim again. And now that Pa knows, I don't have to worry about telling him and Ma myself anymore.

Gert must be really upset about fighting with Pa, because today she forgot her lunch. It was just bread and cheese, but it was food. When I got home from school at noon, Ma asked me to go over to Spadina to the factory and take it to her. She said I'd have just enough time to get there and back to school if I walked fast, and she gave me a lunch for myself to eat there, too, with the other girls.

When I got to the factory, Mr. Tulchinsky, the supervisor, was really nasty to me. When I asked for Gert, he said, "Who's Gert? All these @*#!@?! look the same to me." And he wouldn't let me in to talk to Gert or Sophie or Dora, or even to Uncle Bertzik, who must have been in his office in the back. He just grabbed the lunch from me and said he'd give it to Gert when he had the time, and told me to scram. Dora was sitting at a machine near the door and she looked up and saw I was there, but when she tried to say something, Mr. Tulchinsky just swore at her and told her to get back to work. So she did.

I had to eat my lunch on the steps outside the building by myself. I didn't even have a glass of water to go with it. My mouth felt like a desert all afternoon.

I've been to the factory before, of course, but I never really thought about it. It was just my Uncle

Bertzik's pants factory. Hezekiah Q. Fortnum and Company. But now that Benny's always talking about unions and things, I paid more attention. I guess it really isn't a very nice place to work. It's so noisy with all those sewing machines going all the time. I had to shriek at Mr. Tulchinsky to get him to hear me. And there are no windows and it's very dark except for the lights right over the machines, and the ladies who work there have to sit in a long row and keep sewing for hours and hours to keep up with the rest or else they get fired. They can't even go to the toilet if they feel like it until the supervisor says they can have a break. Sophie says they get paid for each piece they finish, but if they make a mistake they have to pay for it themselves, and if they make too many mistakes, they lose as much as they make and have nothing to take home. And if they get sick or something and can't work, Uncle Bertzik just fires them. It happened to Sophie's friend Ettie last week. Sophie says she thinks that's fair, because it's a factory, not a hospital. But I don't know. Maybe Benny is right about them needing a union.

Sophie and Dora and Gert have to go there and sew the same seam all day long, while I go to school and have fun doing spelling and making sundresses and learning things. I guess I'm lucky. It makes me feel so guilty.

I had a perfect score in arithmetic today. And Miss Douglas liked my story about spring. It's about a poor downtrodden maid who takes the children out to the park on the first warm day of spring and meets a hobo who turns out to be a handsome millionaire in disguise, and they live happily ever after in a little brown house.

June 1

I expected Gert to mope around about Chaim just like Sophie did last fall when Pa stopped her from marrying Steven. She did for a while, but now she isn't moping at all. I wonder why not. It makes me worry. I know she's not sneaking out at night anymore, but she is spending a lot of time after work over at Ida Rothstein's house.

Or so she says. If you ask me, Gert doesn't really like Ida all that much and just lets Ida think she's her friend so Ida will share her clothes with her. Oh well, as long as I don't really know what Gert's doing myself, I guess it's not really any of my business.

June 4

Benny was over with a big bruise on his forehead, and this time it wasn't his pa. Last night he went with the men from the belt factory to a rally in

Trinity Park. It was for unemployed people. Benny says there were hundreds and hundreds of people there, and there were speeches about how the government does everything for the rich *goyim* like themselves and never does anything for poor people or Jews or other foreigners. Benny says a policeman came up and interrupted one of the speeches to ask what was going on, and the man who was talking said it was a public park and they had a right to be there and they just wanted to have a peaceful rally. The policeman said, "Oh, you do, do you?" and walked off. But he must have gone to make a phone call, because a few minutes later a whole bunch of policemen drove up on motorcycles and then marched into the park right up to where the people were speaking and tried to stop them. The crowd started to get mad because they weren't doing anything wrong, and one man ended up hitting a policeman in the face, right beside Benny. The policeman fell over and got trampled. Benny trampled him, too. He couldn't help it, he says, because people behind him were pushing. Then everyone started fighting, and Benny got his bruise.

Benny said he was just trying to get out of there as fast as he could. But he sure seemed to be happy about the fighting, and he is very proud of that bruise. He says he can't wait for the next rally, and he said I should come, too. Does he think I'm crazy?

He told me one good thing, though. His pa was right. The man from the coat factory decided not to charge Uncle Max for sticking the scissors into him. Thank goodness.

June 12

It was really warm yesterday, so Pa decided to get the truck up and running and take us all for a picnic at Balmy Beach. It's a public beach, so we knew for sure there wouldn't be any of those *No Jews Allowed* signs like we saw last summer. Lots of people from the community go there all the time.

When we got there, we decided to go into the water for a swim, but there was nowhere to change. Ma put towels over the truck windows and Gert and Dora and Molly and I took turns changing in there while Ma took Hindl over to a picnic table to change her there.

While she was doing it, a woman sitting at a table nearby was making very loud comments about how disgusting it was. Really! I would have been mortified if I wasn't so angry.

That lady was so nasty, and she went on and on. She said she certainly never expected to see naked children in her park in her own neighbourhood. It may be her neighbourhood, but it's certainly not her park. She told the other ladies that in her opinion, these unmannerly kikes with their naked children and their disgusting foreign ways should stick to their own parts of the city and not pollute nice British neighbourhoods with their lax manners and smelly foods. She made sure she said it loud enough for us all to hear, too. Of course Ma didn't understand what she was saying, but she could tell the lady was talking about us and she made Sophie tell her what it was even though Pa didn't want her to. When Sophie told her, Ma was really upset, and she made Pa take us home right away. We didn't even stay long enough to have our picnic.

How could that woman be so mean? Hindl is just a little girl, and she's adorable, not disgusting. And we weren't eating anything the least bit smelly, unless you count the pickled herring, and I like the smell of pickled herring. And we had just as much right to be there as she did. It makes me so, so mad.

June 13

I told Benny about what happened at Balmy Beach, and he got mad, too. He says no one can push the Jews around and get away with it. He says the boxing match last week proved it.

I know what he means, because everybody was talking about it — even Pa, and he never pays any attention to sports or any of the news. The match was in New York, at Yankee Stadium. An American boxer named Max Baer won over a boxer from Germany, Max Schmeling — and he did it with a Mogen David on his boxing trunks! Actually wearing a Jewish star! He did it because his grandfather is Jewish, and he wanted to show everybody how proud he is of his heritage. Benny says that'll show Hitler and those Germans. Benny thinks we Jews shouldn't let anybody push us around ever.

I think he's right. The next time a lady talks like that about my family, I'm going to give her a piece of my mind. I told Benny I would, and he said good for me. I hope I'll be brave enough to do it.

June 15

Gert is still seeing Chaim. I saw her with him in the park around the corner yesterday, and they were smooching, right out in public. What can she be thinking of? Has she lost her mind completely? I am so worried about her, and I can't tell Ma or Pa, I just can't. I'm too scared. Well, at least Gert isn't pinching me all the time. I guess she has other things on her mind. I wonder if Chaim likes being pinched, because if he keeps on being around her, he better get used to it.

June 20

Now that the farms are starting to have lettuce and things to sell, Pa is back driving the truck again. It's what he really likes to do, and he's always happier in the summer when he's doing it. I'm so happy for him. Of course it means having to pay for the gas, which Pa says is still pretty expensive even if it's a lot less than it used to be, because everyone is so poor now that they try not to drive anywhere. But even after the gas, there'll still be enough money for everything and Ma won't have to keep going to Uncle Bertzik. And it also means we get salad for lunch again, instead of just plain sour cream and cottage cheese.

School will be over next week. I can hardly wait. I like school, I really do, but not when it's so nice out and it gets so hot in the classroom. Today I was dying from the heat and I asked Miss Douglas if I could open the window. She said I could and I tried, but I couldn't reach up high enough and Miss Douglas had to get Melvin Krasner to do it. I hate being so short. If I hadn't been put forward a grade when I was in Junior Two, I wouldn't be smaller than everyone else. It's so unfair. I can't help it if I'm smart.

June 25

Benny isn't in the band anymore. His ma noticed how filthy his tuxedo was and she washed it and it shrank, so he had to quit.

June 27

It was Hindl's birthday today. She's five now. We couldn't afford any presents, of course. But Ma made a nice cake, and I ripped a page out of one of my school scribblers and I drew a picture of a doll and got Molly to draw some dolly clothes, and then Ma cut them out with those little tabs like real paper dolls have, and Hindl was thrilled. She and Molly played with the doll all afternoon, and they didn't even mind that the doll and the clothes had the lines for writing crossing them all over.

June 28

I've been promoted to Senior Four! It'll be my last year at Egerton Ryerson. It's hard to believe that I'll soon be going to high school and I'll be further in school than anybody else in the family ever went.

Pa had hardly any school in the old country, just *cheder* to learn his prayers and things, and even Ma stopped when she was twelve. So did Sophie because Ma and Pa needed her to go out to work, and she thinks she knows everything and is always telling me what to do. Today she wanted to make me memorize the names of all the capital cities of the provinces in Canada, and when I told her I already knew them because of Miss Douglas she made me say them all. Sometimes I think I liked it better when she was moping instead of going to Jewish Juniors meetings all the time.

I got *A*s in almost everything but I nearly failed Domestic Science. It's not my fault. I enjoyed making the blancmange and then the chocolate blancmange in the cooking part, and I loved the smell when we baked bread. But I have to admit I did sort of make a mess of my flannelette underpants. Even Ma couldn't fix the seams after I was finished with them, and she's the best sewer in the whole world. We had to use them for dusting rags. I wish I could sew like Ma does but I just can't. Miss Hayter wouldn't let me sew on the machine until I got my seams straight in hand-sewing, so I never did, so of course I never got to sew up my sundress, which is why I almost failed. It's so unfair. Can I help it if I can't sew?

Miss Hayter said I might as well take the pieces home, and Ma says she'll sew it for me. She'll make it look so beautiful. It's going to be a beautiful sundress, even if it is backless and sleeveless. Well, at least I won't look like a boy in it.

Myrtle MacDonald got an *A* in sewing as well as everything else, so she got to be top girl. The prize was a Mama Doll. That's a pretty good prize, I guess, if you like playing with baby things. Although I have to admit it's a very beautiful doll.

July 5

What a terrible day! I was looking after Molly and Hindl this aft while Ma was over visiting Auntie Rayzel. They were playing with Hindl's paper doll in the backyard, and instead of being the maid again, I was sitting up in the pear tree reading a wonderful book that I got from St. Chris called *The Secret Garden* and I guess I must have got completely caught up in it, because when I came to the end of a chapter and looked around, Molly was playing by herself. We looked all over the house and up and down the street but Hindl wasn't anywhere and I was really, really worried and I felt so awful and Molly couldn't stop crying. That was when Ma came home from Uncle Bertzik and Auntie Rayzel's house. She got hysterical and I started to cry, too, and say it was all my fault and everyone was in a panic.

And then Hindl came toddling up the street all by herself, happy as a clam. Ma grabbed her and hugged her and everyone was screaming and shrieking at her and crying and of course Hindl started to cry, too.

After we all calmed down, Hindl handed Ma a piece a paper. It was a note. It was from the play-room ladies at St. Chris and it said, *Dear Mrs. Hindell: Your daughter would like to be a member of our club. We'll be so pleased if you let her. Yours sincerely, Miss Jones and Miss Macintosh.*

I guess Hindl got bored with her dolly and went down to St. Chris all by herself to play with all the toys they have there in the playroom, like she did last week when I took her with me while I changed my book. Imagine!

Ma was really embarrassed by the note. She said Miss Jones and Miss Macintosh must think she's a terrible mother, because what sort of mother would let a four-year-old wander in the streets all by herself? I reminded Ma that Hindl is five now. But I feel so bad, because it wasn't Ma's fault, it was mine, and I told her so, too, and she told me it wasn't. I love Ma.

Well, at least the playroom ladies don't really

know who Ma is, because when Hindl told the ladies her name they must have thought it was her last name and not her first. I guess they've never heard of anyone called Hindl. Maybe I should teach her to use her English name. The playroom ladies wouldn't think Helen was a last name.

Ma told Hindl she was never to go back to St. Chris ever again. That way they'll never find out what our last name really is. She can't even go to the library. Poor Hindl.

July 9

Benny says if I want to show people like that nasty lady at Balmy Beach last month, then I have to come with him to a rally. It's going to be this Tuesday and it's a protest against Hitler. I told him I'd go. I want to go, but I'm really scared.

Benny said it's going to be like a parade and we're going to march with the Cloakmakers Union and nothing bad will happen. But I'm not sure I believe him, not after what happened at that last rally he told me about. That's why I said I'd go. I figure that if fighting or anything awful happens, then maybe Benny won't get mixed up in it if I'm there because he'll have to look after me and that'll keep him out of it. I hope.

Of course it's much too hot for my reefer coat now. Benny told me that if I wear a pair of his pants instead of a skirt and hide my hair under a cap, I'll still look just like a boy. It made me so mad I almost decided to let him go by himself. But I really am worried what he might do if I'm not there. And I really do want to show that nasty woman in the park. So I guess I'll go, even if it is scary.

July 10

Pa says I have to go with Sophie and Syd to Belle Ewart next week, and he's going to send Hindl with me, so Ma can have a bit of a rest. Sophie and Syd are already paying for the cottage — that really means that Ma and Pa are paying for Sophie out of Sophie's work money — and they say the people who own the cottage will put in a cot for Hindl and me and let us stay for free. I'm supposed to look after Hindl all day while Sophie and Syd are having fun. I guess it's a punishment for losing track of Hindl the other day, but I'm kind of glad because it means Pa still trusts me enough to look after her. Pa is really nice inside even if he hides it sometimes.

Sophie and Syd are going to Belle Ewart because Ma and Pa said they wouldn't let Sophie go anywhere like Wasaga Beach where she'll meet *shayget-*

zes. Sophie got mad and said she didn't want to go to Wasaga Beach and she didn't want to have anything to do with *shaygetzes*. She sure won't at Belle Ewart, because only Jewish people go there.

July 11

Benny brought some pants and a cap over. I told Ma we were going for a walk and then I snuck in the cellar door and put them on while Benny waited outside. Pants feel very strange. I kind of like them. Isn't that awful?

We walked down Spadina past Uncle Bertzik's factory to Clarence Square where the little park is, where the march was starting. There were hundreds and hundreds of people there in all sorts of different groups — Jewish groups and unions and even communists and people like that, and they all had big banners to march behind and signs for people to carry. Our banner said *Cloakmakers Protest Against Pogroms in Germany*. Benny told me that a pogrom is when people come into a place and try to kill all the Jews there just for being Jewish. It happened in Russia a while back, and now it's beginning to happen in Germany. How can people be so evil?

A man handed me a sign to carry that said *Cloakmakers Protest Against Destruction of Trade Unions in*

Germany. I didn't want to carry it, because Pa and Uncle Bertzik are always saying trade unions are bad for everybody. But Benny reminded me that we were marching with the Cloakmakers, which is a union, after all, and I remembered what it was like in the factory that day Mr. Tulchinsky yelled at me — and anyway, I was in disguise, so I took the sign.

I sure hope nobody I know saw me. What would Uncle Bertzik think? What would Rivka Goldstein think?

We marched up Spadina and over to Queen's Park where the big government building is, and then there were all kinds of speeches, and lots of people shouting "Down with Hitler" and things like that. It made me feel so good to see so many people standing up for Jews. There were also some people who got mad at all the rest of us and they were shouting that Hitler is a great man and good for everybody and who did we think we were anyway? It made lots of people in the protest angry, but nobody hit anybody else, thank goodness. At least I didn't see anybody hit anyone else. There were lots of police around, which is probably why.

It was very, very exciting. It was so exciting that I let Benny talk me into putting on the pants again and going to watch the Orange Parade tomorrow. I must be completely *meshugge*.

Benny and I walked down to Queen and Bathurst yesterday to watch the Orange Parade. I thought there were lots of people marching in the protest, but there were thousands and thousands more in the Orange Parade. It took almost three whole hours for the parade to go by us. There were cars with people waving and band after band after band and there were hundreds and hundreds of policemen and firemen and others marching and singing songs like "The Maple Leaf Forever." It made me proud to be part of a British country and a British citizen.

But then one of the marchers going by in a really fancy uniform and a hat with feathers saw me looking at his hat and he gave me a nasty look and said, "What ya staring at, ya little runt kike? Go back where ya come from." It made me feel awful. It was worse than that lady at Balmy Beach.

Benny said he wasn't surprised. He says the people in the Orange lodges are all *anti-semits*. They are people who are proud of being Irish and they think that anyone who isn't Irish is nobody. The worst thing is, they run the whole city — the police department and the fire department and the streetcars and everything. Even the mayor is an Orangeman.

Yesterday I felt so good about the protest, but

now I'm not so sure. If there are so many Orange-men and they run everything and they're all like that man in the parade and that lady at the beach, then what difference can some people marching make? And why are they so worried about Hitler in Germany when things are so bad right here in Toronto? How can the world be so awful?

I really didn't *have* to wear Benny's pants yesterday — there were even girls marching in the parade, Orange girls in white dresses. But I guess I'm glad Benny made me wear them, because what if someone told Pa or Ma or Sophie I was there?

July 24

I decided not to take my scribbler to Belle Ewart since we were all sleeping in the same room. I certainly don't want Sophie or Syd snooping around in it. If Sophie saw what I wrote about her she'd kill me. Maybe I should find a better hiding place.

Anyway, I'm back now. And I don't have anything to write. Nothing interesting happened at Belle Ewart. *Bupkis.* Nothing at all. Me and Hindl were the only young girls around. Everyone in the cabins near us was at least as old as Sophie, and the girls she and Syd talked to were busy impressing each other with the names and jobs of their boyfriends and their makeup and things and they had no time for me ever. I spent the whole time making sure that Hindl didn't drown or get lost in the woods. Syd brought some cherries with her, which I think was very cruel. Doesn't she remember what happened last year? Anyway, I didn't eat a single one. I am never eating cherries ever again. And I nearly died from the heat. It's been so hot all summer, and I wore my new sundress all the time. I started out wearing a blouse over it, but then I remembered Gert wasn't there so I took it off. No one there said a single thing about my arms. But maybe that's because nobody ever even looked at me. I am so glad to be back home.

July 25

Now I'm *really* worried about Benny, even more than I was before. He told me he went up to Christie Pits last week to watch his friend Harvey Tischler, Harvey the Horseballer, play in a softball game. Harvey is the catcher for the Harbord Playground Juvenile team, which is mostly Jewish boys, and they were playing against a team of mostly *goyishe* boys from a church on Bloor. After the game, he and Harvey were walking down to Bloor through the park and they heard a bunch of people shouting "Hail Hitler." It was a gang of boys, and they surrounded Benny and Harvey, and Benny and Harvey had to push some of them down and take off and run like crazy to save their lives.

Benny says those boys call themselves the Pit Gang. A Jewish boy he knows who lives near there told him they hang out in that park every night and they hate Jews and they think the park and the whole neighbourhood belongs to them.

Benny got so mad that he went and told this man he knows named Al Kaufman all about it. He says Al is a really tough guy from Winnipeg or somewhere. And guess what! He's a hobo! Imagine my own cousin Benny knowing a hobo! Who even knew there are hoboes who are Jewish?

Well, I guess Pa's cousin Yankl is a hobo, sort of, or at least he was the last time we heard from him, so maybe it's not so surprising.

But Al Kaufman is *really* a hobo. He has been riding the rails for years, Benny says — ever since the Depression started. He calls himself the King of the Hoboes and he's been hanging out in the Eppes Essen deli on College with a bunch of other Jewish guys who call themselves the Up-town Gang. Now the King of the Hoboes and the Up-town Gang are planning to go up to the Pits and do something about the Pit Gang, and Benny is planning to be there when it happens.

I tried to get him to say he wouldn't go, but I couldn't. I hope he just stays close to home.

July 28

Benny says the Up-town Gang have put off going up to the Pits because now even worse things are happening at Balmy Beach. He says there's a rumour that a bunch of the boys who live out there have been walking up and down the boardwalk insulting Jews and trying to pick fights with boys or men who look Jewish. They think the Beach belongs to them. A couple of guys have come back with black eyes and bruises.

Ma wants me to get the table ready for Shabbes dinner. I have to go.

August 1

Benny came here yesterday all excited and said he wanted me to look after his money while he went somewhere. I wouldn't take it until he told me where he was going.

He was going to Balmy Beach. He said things have got even worse there. Now the *goyim* have started a club. It's called the Swastika Club. They've been painting swastikas, like the Nazis use in Germany, on rocks all along the boardwalk. They even put a huge swastika sign up in front of the Canoe Club out there at the beach, with *Hail Hitler* on it. Benny says they're such idiots they don't even know how to spell the German word *Heil*.

Benny says Al Kaufman showed his gang a copy of a notice the Swastikas put up on the Canoe Club bulletin board and were putting up around the neighbourhood. Someone, a Jewish man named Abe Nodelman who owns a little store out there, stole one and brought it to him. It said that they wanted to do something about the undesirable visitors coming into their neighbourhood, so they were selling a badge with a swastika on it for 25¢. They want people to wear it on the beach to show how they feel about Jews.

Even worse, yesterday afternoon a bunch of them marched down the boardwalk wearing the badges and singing a song to the tune of "Home on the Range" about how they wanted a home where the Gentiles could roam without hearing any loud Yiddish words. As soon as the Up-towns heard about it they decided to drive out to the beach to do something about it. And Benny wanted to go, too.

I tried to talk him out of it. I even tried to get him to let me wear the pants and come along like I did last time, so I could keep him out of the fighting. But he refused. He said it was no place for a girl, and he started pulling coins and bills out of all his pockets and handing them to me.

I was astonished! It was a small fortune! I asked him where he got it because I was afraid he was gambling or something else bad again. But he said not to worry, it's just his money from the belt factory. His ma makes him keep it for her because if he gives it to her his pa just makes her give it to him and then he goes out and gets drunk. Benny has nowhere safe to keep it except on himself, and he didn't want to get into a fight while he had it.

I took the money. I really didn't have a choice. But now I can't decide if I'm more worried about losing it or having Gert find it or about what might happen to Benny.

August 2

Benny came to get his money and he told me what happened. It's scary, but somehow, I always feel better after I write it all down.

There were about sixty or seventy Jewish boys and men, and they all crammed into some poultry trucks from the market. A lot of them had pipes and boards, and when they got out to Balmy Beach they went right up to the Canoe Club. There was no *Hail Hitler* sign out front anymore. The Swastika Gang must have heard they were coming and got rid of it.

Anyway, Al Kaufman had a large dog with him, and he marched right past the refreshment stand and onto the club grounds looking for other swastikas. He couldn't find any, thank goodness, but the Canoe Club was full of *goyim* with broom handles and lacrosse sticks and other weapons, because they heard the Jews were coming. For a while, everyone just stood around looking mad and waiting for someone to make the first move. Then the police showed up and cleared the grounds of the Canoe Club. There was a dance going on inside, but the police told everyone there to go home. The *goyim* all left, but the Jewish guys went wandering up and down the boardwalk and up and down the streets close to the shore looking for swastikas. There weren't any, so they got in their trucks and came back home. But Benny says they're planning to go back again.

I wish they wouldn't. If Benny and the other Jewish boys start fighting, who knows what might happen? I am very, very scared, and I can't tell Ma or Dora or anybody. They'd just say it's none of our business and not to worry. They wouldn't understand.

August 3

I took Molly and Hindl for a walk over to Bellevue Park, and I found a *Tely* newspaper that someone left on a bench. One of the hoboes must have been using it for a blanket. Anyway, there was a picture of the swastika and the big *Hail Hitler* on the Canoe Club and other pictures of swastikas on people's shirts, right there on the front page. Seeing it in the paper made it seem so real. It's so hard to believe that this is happening right here in Toronto, right where I live.

August 4

Benny says the Swastika Gang keep saying they aren't anti-Semitic, just people who want to keep the beaches clean, and they're only using the swastika because it's an ancient symbol that means brother-hood and good luck. Benny says it just proves that all the *goyim* are *anti-semits*, but I don't know. Maybe they're right about the swastika. I remember looking at *The Just-So Stories* by Kipling at the St. Chris library one day last winter — I used to love those stories when I was little. Anyway, there was something that looked a lot like one of those swastikas on the cover, and that book has nothing to do with Nazis or Jews. It's just about cute animals. I told that to Benny and he said maybe so, but the boys in the Swastika Gang sure hate Jews, or why else would they put up a *Hail Hitler* sign? I guess he's right.

A lot of Jewish unions and clubs and things are planning to have their picnics for the long weekend at Balmy Beach, just to show the Swastikas, and Benny says the mayor got Bert Ganter, the boy who's the leader of the Swastika Club, to promise that there won't be any marches or swastikas. I'm so glad the mayor wants to keep things calm even though he's an Orangeman. But Benny thinks that a lot of the boys from the east end will be on the Beach on Sunday wearing swastikas anyway. Al Kaufman and a bunch of other Jewish guys are definitely planning to be there, and so is Benny. He even gave me all his money again.

If Benny's going, so am I. I'll tell Ma that Rivka invited me to go with her to visit her cousin on Crawford Street or something, but really, I'll go to the Beach. I'm going to wear the pants and the hat and go on the streetcar. I borrowed some money from Benny to pay the fare. He doesn't know about it, of course, but I'll pay him back some day for sure. Once I'm there at the beach I can find Benny and see if I can keep him away from the fighting.

I am still scared, but I have to do it. I have to.

It was just awful at the beach. There were all sorts of *goyishe* boys marching up and down the boardwalk wearing the little swastika badges. Some of then even had swastikas painted on their shirts, and there were even *goyishe* girls with swastikas pinned on their bathing suits. Once I saw two bunches of them meet, and they all said "Hail" and stuck their arms out just like the Nazis in Germany do — I saw them do it in the Movietone news.

There were also gangs of Jewish boys, and a lot of them had maple leaves painted on their shirts. Benny says they wanted to show they were just Canadians like everyone else. The Jews and the *goyim* were jostling each other and calling each other names as they passed on the boardwalk, and once I saw a big group of Jews surround a couple of *goyim* and tear their shirts off and then run away and hide behind a house across the street. I just tried to look invisible.

It took me a while but I finally found Benny. He and a few other boys were just about to rip a shirt off a *goy,* and I ran up and yelled at him to stop before he got killed or something and the *goy* got away. Benny was really angry at me for being there. He told me to go home, but I refused unless he came with me, and he wouldn't.

We were arguing right there on the boardwalk when we heard singing and shouting. It was a bunch of men coming along the boardwalk, wearing big swastikas on their shirts and humming "Home on the Range." They didn't sing the words about Gentiles being free to roam, but we all knew what they meant. When Benny heard what they were humming, he got even angrier than he was already, and he rushed over and grabbed one of the shirts and ripped it right off and ran away with it. The *goyim* saw me standing there and they looked like they wanted to kill me and I was so scared I couldn't even make myself run. Luckily, a couple of policemen showed up and

Later

I had to stop writing because Ma sent me to Koslov's to get some salt. She's making pickles today and the summer kitchen is so, so hot. Where was I? Oh yes, the policemen.

The policemen ordered the *goyim* to take the swastikas off, and a crowd of Jews gathered around and started shouting, "Take them off, take them off." But the *goyim* refused. One of them told the police it was a free country and they weren't doing anything wrong and if they were then the police should arrest them, but the police didn't. More and more Jews were gathering around us and everyone was shouting. The policemen looked worried, and one of them told the *goyim* they should be more reasonable, because their actions were threatening the safety of women and children, and there was no point having a riot over some lousy shirts. Finally, they agreed. I don't know if the police talked them into it or they were just scared of the crowd. One of them shouted that they'd do it, but just for the sake of the women and children. Then they took the swastikas off and went away and things got a little calmer.

That was when Benny came back. He said he was hiding behind the boathouse. He was worried about me, he said, but he figured that he'd better not show himself and that I was safe as long as the policemen were there. But he said that maybe we should go home after all. I was so glad I almost hugged him.

We were walking up to Queen Street to get the streetcar when a car stopped and a man asked Benny where he was going and told us to get in, because it was too dangerous for us to be walking by ourselves in that neighbourhood. I didn't want to because the car was full of strange men, but Benny said it was okay. The men in the car were Al Kaufman and some of the Up-town Gang. Benny told me later. They didn't look like hoboes at all. At least they were a lot cleaner than Cousin Yankl or those men in the park.

We got in with the men and drove down Queen, and then we stopped in front of a store a few blocks later — the Black and White Confectionery. Al Kaufman and the other men got out and told Benny and me to stay in the car, and they were walking toward the store when some men came out. It was the men who were humming "Home on the Range" on the boardwalk! Benny hunkered down in the car so they couldn't see him. Later, Al Kaufman told us that two of those men were Mackay and Ganter. They are the leaders of the Swastika Gang and the Black and White is their headquarters.

Al Kaufman told them he was there as a representative of Rabbi Sachs and the Up-town boys, and he wanted to know about the Swastika Club. Did they want to stir up racial prejudice? They said no, they just wanted to make the Beaches cleaner. Al said he understood — which really surprised me, but I kept my mouth shut. Al said the ones who cause most of the trouble are greenhorns from the old country who don't know about proper manners.

I don't know why he was being so nice, but I'm glad he was, because it seemed to work. There wasn't a fight. They all shook hands and then Al Kaufman and the other Jews got back in the car and we headed home. Once he was back in the car, Al said he knows those guys are *anti-semits* and he was trying to calm things down because that's what the rabbi wanted, but he's going to keep an eye on them. Benny agreed. I hope they are wrong.

It's funny, but on the boardwalk all the boys seemed to be having a good time — the *goyishe* boys *and* the Jews. Especially Benny. If it wasn't for the swastikas and the police, it was just like they were playing street hockey or something. I hated it.

I got Al Kaufman to let me out on the corner on Nassau far away from our house, but Gert saw me anyway. She wanted me to tell her who the men were and where I was, but I refused. She said she'd tell Ma and Pa and I said maybe that wasn't a good idea because I'm not the only one with a secret, and she got all red and stomped off. Thank goodness. But now I'm never going to be able to tell Ma and Pa about her and Chaim. What an awful day.

August 11

It's so, so hot. Pa drove out to buy some tomatoes from the farmers yesterday and he came back with almost none. The farmers told him it's been so hot this summer that half the tomatoes growing in the Niagara peninsula have been ruined by the sun. If there are no tomatoes for Pa to buy and bring back to the Fruit Terminal, we'll have even less money than usual. I don't know how we're going to make it through next winter.

The worst thing is, I've used up almost all this scribbler. Where will I get the money for a new one? I suppose I could have borrowed it from Benny before I gave him his money back on Tuesday. Maybe I could ask him and he'd lend it to me anyway.

August 13

I haven't seen Benny since he came to get his money back, but today he came around to tell me he's been hanging out with the Up-towns. Al Kaufman figures that what he said to the Swastikas must have worked, because they had a meeting at city hall with the mayor and some rabbis and other people, and the Swastika Club agreed to change its name. They're still going to have a club to stop people from behaving badly at the beach, but without any swastikas — and they say anyone of any religion can join. I am so, so relieved. I just wish Benny wouldn't hang out with those tough men. Al Kaufman seems nice, I guess, but he is a hobo, and they don't call him King of the Hoboes for nothing.

Benny came because he wanted to invite me to go

with him and Harvey Tischler to a softball game up at Christie Pits tomorrow night. It's a playoff game between the Harbord Juniors and St. Peter's, the Catholic church at Bathurst and Bloor. Benny said that since Harvey Tischler is on the Harbord Juveniles, he knows some of the older guys on the Juniors and he wants them to win. Anyway, it's a mostly Jewish team and Benny says we have to support our own guys and everyone is going and I have to go to, for the sake of the Jews.

I hate sports and Benny knows it. But it's so hot in the house now, especially when it starts to get dark, and Gert is hanging around me and giving me dirty looks all the time because she's worried I'll say something about Chaim, so I said I'd go. Benny said good, because the more of us there are then the safer it'll be for everyone, if I know what he means. Then he winked at me. I don't know what he means, but now I'm really worried all over again.

I forgot to ask Benny about money for the scribbler. Darn.

August 14

It's very late, but I'm so upset, and maybe writing about it will calm me down like it did last time.

Benny came around with Harvey Tischler to get

me, and Harvey nearly died laughing when he saw me in a dress for the first time. Harvey is a strange person. At least he smells a little better now than he did in the winter.

During the game, things were pretty calm for a long time. It was a pretty big crowd, and the people were yelling all kinds of things about no-good shee-nies and *meshuggeneh goyim* to support the teams, but nobody really seemed to be very upset about anything. It was more like teasing.

But then the lacrosse game that was going on across the park finished and all the people who were watching it came over to see the end of the softball game. They were all *goyim*, and there seemed to be hundreds of them, and they all started yelling nasty things in a nasty way. One man beside me shouted, "Let's go, boys! Let's show these kikes who's boss around here!" He shouted right in my ear and gave me a really nasty look. It was getting really scary.

It frightens me again just thinking about it. I have to calm down.

All during the game, there was a bunch of *goyishe* boys standing out by the left fielder where everyone in the crowd could see them. They were carrying a big piece of cloth, black with white markings on it, and towards the end of the game, they started to unroll it very slowly, bit by bit, while the *goyim* cheered and egged them on. At the end of the ninth inning, the score was tied, so the teams kept on playing, and those boys kept on rolling and unrolling their piece of cloth, just teasing, never quite showing the whole thing. After Harbord got a hit and tied the score again, the crowd booed really loudly, and that was when the boys in left field finally unrolled their cloth all the way. When it was all unrolled, it turned out to be a long black sweater coat with a white swastika sewed onto it! What a nerve!

The crowd went wild. The *goyim* all cheered and said "Hail Hitler." Benny wanted to go right over and try to rip it out of their hands, but Harvey and I managed to hold him back and talk him out of it. By the time we calmed him down a little there was a whole big gang of *goyim* standing around the banner so Benny and the other Jewish boys couldn't get close even if they wanted to.

The ump told everyone to calm down and he started the game again. The next Harbord boy at bat got another hit, and Harbord won the game and the crow booed even more. As soon as the game was over, the boys standing around the swastika held it up high and rushed onto the field with it, chanting, "Down with Jews! Hail Hitler!" They surrounded the Harbord team and Benny and I got pushed right into the middle of it. They were shoving and screaming and yelling and I was so scared I couldn't even think or move or anything. Harvey and Benny tried to hold them back, and Benny shouted that there was a defenceless little girl there and they were cowards to pick on her. He meant me, and he was right. I was feeling very defenceless. Finally some of the *goyim* heard him and saw me and cleared a path for us. The rest of the Harbord team all huddled around me because they were outnumbered about fifty to one and about to be clobbered, and we all got up the hill and out of the park and ran away from there down Christie Street as fast as we could.

After we got to Bloor, Benny tried to talk me into walking home by myself while he went back to the park, but the other boys said there were too many *goyim* there and talked him out of it. But he sure was angry.

I can still feel my heart going like crazy. I bet I won't be able to sleep.

August 15

Benny was just here and he was even madder than he was last night. Sometime last night after the game was over and everyone left, someone painted a huge swastika and the words *Hail Hitler* on the Willow-vale Park Clubhouse in the Pits. He says it's still there. First it was Germany, and then Balmy Beach, and now Christie Pits. It's getting closer and closer all the time.

They painted *Hail* instead of *Heil,* just like they did at Balmy Beach, so I wondered if it might be the same people. But Benny says he thinks it was the Pit Gang just being copycats. They think they own the park, and they're too dumb to even know they were copying a mistake.

Benny says they're not the only ones, either. The papers say there was a swastika rally in Kitchener last night to support Hitler. Kitchener is out in the country near where Pa goes sometimes to buy cabbages and things in the fall. Benny says it's not surprising, since a lot of German people live there. Kitchener even used to be called Berlin, just like that big city in Germany — until the Great War started and they had to change the name. Mackay, one of the men from the Swastikas that Al Kaufman talked to, went to the rally there and made a speech, and Benny says it proves he was a Nazi after all. Ganter was supposed to go too, but the papers say he never showed up.

The next game in the Harbord–St. Peter's series is tomorrow. Benny says he's planning to be there. A lot of Jewish boys are — not to cause trouble, just to protect the team. He told me not to come this time, because things are getting bad and it's way too dangerous. I don't want to go. It was so scary last night. But if we don't go out and stand up for ourselves, it will end up being just like in Germany. I have to be there.

I decided not to ask Benny for the money for a new scribbler. I know that every penny he has goes to buy food and things for his ma and his little brothers, and he never ever buys anything for himself, not even a new shirt or pants, and he could sure use those. And if he did lend me money, Molly and Hindl need things just as much as Willie and Joe do. I can do without a scribbler for a while, even if I do like writing about everything.

August 17

There are only a few pages left in the scribbler, and there's so much to tell. I'm going to have to write really small.

Anyway, what a night! I went to the game by myself. Ma thought I was at St. Chris, but I wasn't. When I got to the Pits, I was glad to see that some-one had painted out the sign on the clubhouse roof. But there was still a big dark patch and you could tell the sign had been there, which is almost as bad.

There was a huge crowd, and it seemed to be half Jews and half *goyim* and it was very, very tense. As I came down the slope to the softball diamond, I heard a gang of *goyishe* boys out past centre field shouting, "Go, St. Peter's! Get the Jews! Hail Hitler!" But then a bunch of big Jewish men came over to them and told them to shut up or else. I recognized one of them — it was Al Kaufman. One of the *goyim* kept right on shouting about Hitler, and one of the Jewish men punched him right in the face. His friends had to take him away with a bleeding nose. As they left the park, they shouted that they'd be back and the Jews better watch out.

That was when Benny noticed I was there and came over and yelled at me and told me to go home. It was just like at the beach. But this time I guess he knew he wasn't ever going to get me to leave, because he gave up almost right away. He just got me to promise to stick close to him and be careful. I looked him right in the eye and I said, "You too, Benny," and he gave me a dirty look and we went down the hill to find a good spot.

As we headed down to the diamond, someone gave Benny a shove and he fell down the hill and rolled right into the cage behind the batter's box. He came up steaming mad and ready to fight. But whoever did it was gone and there was a huge crowd of *goyim* laughing at him. I managed to calm him down and we settled in to watch the game.

We ended up standing in a big group of Jews on the hill beside the diamond. There was a smaller bunch of about thirty *goyim* standing next to us, and in the second inning, they suddenly start chanting, "Hail Hitler, Hail Hitler." The Jews in my group rushed them, and I was standing in the middle of them and got dragged along even though I tried to stay where I was. And then, suddenly, everyone was carrying a weapon! I guess they all had them hidden under their shirt or up their pant legs. A lot of people were jabbing at other people with lead pipes or pieces of wood from fences.

I didn't stop to think, I just tried to get out of there as fast as I could. I wasn't the only one, either. I got pushed up the hill to the edge of the park by a whole big crowd. Once I got to the top I looked back and there was Benny, running after me and telling me to wait for him. He didn't know that there was a gang of five or six *goyishe* boys with sticks and pipes running after *him*. I shouted at him to watch out, and then we both started running as fast as we could. It took us about six blocks, but we finally lost the *goyim*. I was completely out of breath, and I hate to admit it, but it was kind of exciting.

I need to sharpen my pencil.

Okay, it's sharp now. I really shouldn't be writing so much, because I really am running out of pages.

After we both got our breath back, Benny tried to talk me out of going back. But there was no way I was leaving. Sure, it was scary, but I was excited, and it was important. There had to be as many Jews there as possible so we could all protect each other. When I said that to Benny he gave me the strangest look, like he didn't know who I was. He wasn't the only one. What was I thinking? I must have been completely out of my head.

By the time we made it back to the park, it was already the next inning and we heard people shouting "Hail Hitler" again and we saw a bunch of the Jewish boys get surrounded and hit a few times. There was a policeman there by then, and he was trying to calm things down, and I guess he did a little. But there was only one of him and a huge crowd of people who were getting angrier with every passing minute. Things were really tense all through the rest of the game, with people shouting insults and shoving each other, and I was beginning to think maybe I shouldn't have come back. But a few more policemen showed up and nothing really serious happened. Finally, just when it was getting dark, the St. Peter's shortstop caught a fly ball from the last Harbord hitter and St. Peter's won 6–5 and all the Jews booed and all the *goyim* cheered like crazy.

The game was over, and I was so glad nothing

serious had happened. But no one seemed to be leaving. Everyone was just milling around on the field and muttering, like they were waiting for something bad to happen. That was when a bunch of *goyim* standing on the little hill out past centre field spread out a large white blanket with a black swastika sewn onto it — just like that sweater coat the last time, but even bigger.

Everyone started shouting, "The swastika! Look at the swastika!" A bunch of Jewish boys tried to rush the *goyim* to get the blanket. Some of the Harbord boys who were still on the field grabbed bats and started swinging, and suddenly, everyone had their sticks and pipes out and they were all fighting. Some Jewish boys got hold of the swastika blanket and ripped it to shreds, but when they tried to hold up the shreds to show the crowd, they got pushed down and trampled. Everywhere around me people were punching each other and hitting each other with sticks and things.

Benny must have decided things were getting out of control, because he said we had to leave right away and he grabbed my hand and started to pull me through the crowd. By then I couldn't wait to get out of there. I nearly got hit three or four times, but we made it to the edge. As we were standing there trying to catch our breath, one of Al

Kaufman's gang came running up the hill, heading for a car he had parked there. He told Benny that Al was sending him to go down to Spadina and round up more Jewish guys, because the fighting was only going to get worse. Benny asked him to take me with him, to get me away. By then I was back to being myself again, and I was glad to go. Everyone in the park seemed to be completely out of their senses, and they were attacking each other without even seeming to notice or care which side the other person was on. There all had crazy *meshuggeneh* looks in their eyes and there were people shrieking and yelling and there was was blood everywhere. It was awful.

I tried to get Benny to come with me, but I knew he wouldn't. I saw him head back down into the Pits as we drove off. I hope he's okay. I'm really, really worried. Why doesn't he come over and let me know?

The Up-town man drove really fast and stopped the car in front of the Goblin restaurant at College and Spadina. He told me to find my own way home, and then he climbed onto the top of the car and started shouting, *"Gevalt, me shlugt yidn!"* Suddenly the street was full of men, pouring out of the delis and other places and asking who was beating up Jews. When the Up-town man told them, some of

the men ran out into the street and stopped the cars
and trucks that were passing, and then as many men
as could jumped into each of the cars and trucks and
told the drivers to head for the Pits. The Up-town
man was still shouting when I left to go home. I
snuck in the cellar door, and no one knew I was late
except Gert and she won't tell or else.

I hardly slept all night. I kept seeing the crazy
looks on everyone's face and those sticks and pipes
crashing into people heads.

Where is Benny? What's happened to him?

After Midnight

Benny finally showed up. He has a lot of awful
bruises and he says he has a very bad headache, but
he seems to be okay. *Kayn aynhoreh*. And now I
know what happened after I left.

After he saw me drive off with the Up-town man,
Benny headed right back into the Pits. He could see
the Jews all gathered together around the Harbord
team to protect the players and each other, because
there were so many *goyim*. He somehow managed to
get through the crowd to where they were and he
says things looked pretty bad for a while. But then
the cars and trucks from Spadina started pulling up,
and the Jewish guys leapt out of them and ran down

the slope and just started attacking whoever was in front of them. Everyone was fighting everyone else. Benny says he picked up a big tree branch someone had knocked down and waded right in himself. He says he hit all sorts of *goyim*. He seems very proud of it, too. I don't know whether to be happy about it or not. He does seem okay, I guess.

Finally, after an hour or so, some policemen on horses showed up, and then a bit later more came on motorcycles, and they all rode into the park and tried to stop the fighting. They did get a lot of people to leave the park, and it looked like everything was over. But the streets around the park were still full of little separate groups of Jews and *goyim*, and every once in a while they'd meet up with each other and the fighting would start again right there on the street. Benny says he could see people standing at their windows inside the houses, staring out and looking frightened.

The motorcycle policemen started patrolling the streets, breaking up the fights, and telling everyone to go home. But as soon as the police left, everyone just went back towards the park again.

On the way there, Benny got hit on the head by a rock, and this guy he knew, Joe Gold, took him to his aunt's house on Christie Street, where she cleaned him up and put on a bandage and told him to go home. But he didn't, of course — he just went right back to the fighting. Honestly! I could kill him!

Back at the Pits, the mounted police and motorcycle police had made a complete circle around the park, which was full of *goyim*, and they wouldn't let anyone else in. As Benny was standing there with a bunch of Jewish boys and staring at the police, he heard a rumour that a Jewish boy had been killed. That got everyone even angrier.

I wonder if it's true. I hope it isn't.

Anyway, Benny said that then more trucks full of Jews showed up and they rushed the police and broke through their lines. Benny went along with them, and ended up fighting with a bunch of *goyim* with blackjacks and steel pipes. He says he gave them as good as he got, which from the looks of his face is pretty good.

The police finally broke up the fight and pushed everyone up the slope of the park and onto the street again. But of course the same thing happened as before. They just kept fighting in the streets around the park again. As Benny was being shoved out of the park by a policeman, he saw another truck show up with more Jews on it. But by then there were lots and lots of police around, and they surrounded the truck and made the driver leave with the Jews still on board. Benny ended up on Christie Street with a few other Jews, with a large group of *goyim* trying to get at them. The police kept rushing at the *goyim* and pushing them back and they finally did.

Finally, by about midnight, things quietened down. Benny got on a truck with some of the Up-town guys and got a lift back to the neighbourhood. As he was walking down Spadina to get home, some cars went by with *goyim* in them shouting "Hail Hitler." Seeing those *anti-semits* coming right into Jewish territory made him really mad, he says, but he was alone, so he hid in the shadows until they were gone.

But he says it's not over yet, because the Up-town Gang is planning to be prepared for Friday night, when the two teams are supposed to meet again at the Pits for the next game of the playoffs. Benny's already picked out a good heavy pipe to bring.

It makes me so furious. He won't be satisfied until he kills someone, or someone kills him. None of them will. I can't believe this is happening to us. To Benny. To me.

August 18

All day yesterday everyone was talking about the riot — even Ma and Pa, and they never pay any attention to the news. I guess you can't blame them.

They can't read the English papers, and we can't afford the Yiddish one. But still, it drives me crazy. Pa always says it's none of his business, because the *goyishe shmendricks* who run things will run them the way they want whether he finds out about it or not. He says that's just the way the world is and always has been and Jews just need to stick to their own places and their own kind and be good Jews and go to *shul* and mind their own business.

I am going to have to write really small now, because there's not much paper left and I still have lots to say. There's so much to tell and so much to think about. Would it be so bad to ask Benny to lend me some money? Yes, it would be. I know it would.

Anyway, we were all sitting on the front porch after supper because it was so hot inside, and Benny came around and told us that the *Tely* says the riot was caused by communist agitators who showed the swastika because they knew it would get people excited. Benny said that's totally ridiculous — why would communists want to show a swastika? The Nazis hate commies and vice versa. Anyway, he knows for sure it was the boys from the Pit Gang because he recognized some of them. Pa gave Benny a nasty look and said that no god-fearing Jew would behave the way the boys did in the park or even be there at all and Benny should be ashamed of himself. My face turned beet red but I certainly didn't want Pa to know I was there, too, so I didn't say anything. Benny tried to argue with Pa and he told Benny he's *meshuggeneh* and he doesn't know anything, just like his pa. I had to drag Benny away before he started yelling at my pa.

Pa has a point, I guess. I was terrified when I was there in the Pits, and maybe it would have been better to just stay out of it and be safe. But would it really be safe? Can you be safe anywhere when people hate you so much just for being Jewish? Shouldn't you try to do something about it? Maybe not fighting, but something. I love Pa, but I think he's wrong. Just as wrong as Benny is for thinking that hitting people with tree branches is the answer.

I took Benny around the corner to the swings in Bellvue Park, and he told me it was only a rumour that a Jewish boy got killed. Thank goodness. But a whole bunch of guys got treated at Western Hospital for head injuries and other things.

Benny also told me he had just been up to Christie Street, where he went to bring Joe Gold's aunt some chocolates to thank her for looking after him. I think he really just went there looking for trouble, but I was too polite to say so. Anyway, he says there was a gang of *goyishe* boys out in the street — little ones no older than me. I gave him a kick in the ankle for that. The boys weren't saying anything much, just trying to look tough and hanging around outside of houses where Jews live and trying to look menacing. As Benny was leaving some boys called him a kike and one threw an apple core at him and then they all took off. He saw them heading off for the Pits and decided to follow them, but when he got there, there were policemen everywhere, and they told him it's a dangerous place for Jews to be, because a bunch of *goyishe* boys with chains and broom handles were there just waiting for trouble. They sent him home.

Benny thinks it's unfair that the *goyim* are allowed in the Pits and he isn't. He says he could even hear chants of "Hail Hitler" coming from the park, and the police weren't doing anything to stop it. But he was by himself again, so he decided that maybe the policemen were right after all, and he left. But he says it'll be a different story tomorrow. Tomorrow, he says, those *anti-semits* will see what Jews are made of.

I didn't even try to talk him out of it. He is completely obsessed and completely *meshugge*. We might as well start planning his funeral. Benny is doomed. Maybe we all are.

There's just one page and the back cover of the scribbler left. I'll have to work hard to squeeze everything in.

The next playoff game has been postponed for a week. I'm so glad. There hasn't been any serious trouble in Christie Pits or anywhere since the night of the last game. Benny is still in one piece, and so is everyone else.

Benny was right. The papers say that it was the Pit Gang that showed the swastika blanket, and some of them have been arrested. Benny says as far as anyone can tell, they're just a bunch of hooligans. They certainly weren't commies and they have no connection to the Nazis in Germany or even to the men out at the Beaches who started the whole swastika thing. They're just mad because Jews have started moving into their neighbourhood and they think it should be just for *goyim*. I'm glad they got arrested and the Jewish people who live there can have some peace. It's their country, too. It's our country, too.

Still, I'm not happy about Benny and his plans. He wants to go to the Pits tonight with a bunch of other boys even if there is no game. He says they just want to show the *goyim* that the park doesn't belong to them. According to Benny, the Jewish boys don't want to start a fight, but if anyone else starts something, then they're ready to die with their boots on like the brave British citizens they are.

They have to, he says, because he knows the police are on the side of the *goyim*. One of his friends from the belt factory was at a meeting at the Labour Lyceum a few nights ago and he heard this man from the CCF, Captain Philpott or something like that, blame the police chief for the riot. The night it happened the chief sent truckloads of cops down to a labour meeting at Trinity Park even though he knew there might be a riot in the Pits. Benny says the chief did it because he's an Orangeman and he hates communists and he doesn't care what happens to Jews.

Well, maybe that captain is right and maybe he isn't. But going off in a gang to the Pits is just going to cause trouble. There must be a better way. There has to be.

And darn darn darn! I've got just a couple of inches left at the bottom of the back cover and then that's it. The end. I have to get a new scribbler. I don't want to stop. I like writing about everything. Even when I write about really scary things I don't feel so scared anymore.

Epilogue

Sally did manage to get another scribbler to write in, a few weeks later. But by that time, she was back in school and busy with homework, and it seemed as if everyone had forgotten all about the riot and the swastikas, including Sally. She never wrote another word about it. In fact, the scary night at Christie Pits was the last outbreak of violence between the Jews and the swastika gangs. Benny and his friends stayed out of trouble at Christie Pits. At the postponed game between Harbord and St. Peter's the next week, only seventy-one people showed up, and there was no trouble. Nobody knows why. St. Peter's won the game, 5–4.

Sally continued to do well at school. She was at the top of her class in Senior Four. Myrtle Mac-Donald came second, and they both went on to Harbord Collegiate, but Sally never did talk to Myrtle. Sally felt guilty about staying in school when times were so tough, but Sophie insisted.

But the Depression didn't get much better, and the lack of money in the family finally ruined Sophie's plan for Sally to go to university and become a lawyer. Instead, she went to work as a receptionist and bookkeeper at a fur coat company on Spadina, Kaufman Brothers and Fine. She modelled fur coats for the customers whenever one of the Mr. Kaufmans or Mr. Fine asked her to, even though she thought she wasn't pretty enough. The customers didn't seem to mind.

While Sally was going to school and modelling coats, Benny kept on working at the belt factory and getting into trouble with his father. He got involved with the Cloakmakers union, and spent a lot of his money at the racetrack and at the bootlegger's. Sally thought it was disgraceful, but even after she made new girlfriends at Harbord, Benny was still her best friend — even if he insisted on always coming over to give her the bad news about Hitler.

Things just got worse and worse for the Jews in Germany, and not many people in Canada seemed to care very much. The government wouldn't even let very many Jews who were trying to get away from Hitler come to Canada. It made Sally very angry.

Then in 1939, World War II began. As soon as Canada joined Great Britain and other Commonwealth countries in the fight against Germany and the Nazis, Benny signed up for the army. He told Sally he wouldn't be able to live with himself if he didn't. She was angry at him for putting himself in danger, but secretly proud of his bravery. He joined the Infantry and died in the raid on Dieppe in August of 1942.

Sally was very upset when she heard that Benny had died. So was Harvey Tischler, Benny's best friend, who had joined the army the same day Benny did. Harvey was so short-sighted that he wasn't able to join a fighting regiment, and he spent the war years in the Service Corps at Camp Borden, north of Toronto, working in the Quartermaster's stores. Sally ran into him on Spadina one afternoon in 1943 while he was on leave, and they had a good time reminiscing about Benny and the band and the events at Christie Pits. Sally decided Harvey didn't smell anywhere near as bad as he once had. A year later, they married.

A year after that, Sally moved with their little baby Benjamin to Alliston, a small village a few kilometres away from Camp Borden, to be near Harv. Sally's parents and sisters were furious with her, especially because no other Jews lived in Alliston and no kosher food was available there. They told her she couldn't manage to live so far away from the community and from her family and her own kind all by herself. A few weeks after she moved, the entire family came up to Alliston on Pa's truck, convinced Sally would have had enough by then and would be willing to pack up her things and come home with them. But she and little Benjy stayed, and she made friends with people in the town and with other army wives. None of them was Jewish. One of them turned out to be Myrtle MacDonald's older sister — a woman Sally especially liked.

After the war, Harvey left the army and joined his father in his jewellery business, playing in bands on evenings and weekends. Sally offered to sing with the bands, but Harvey, who had heard her very high voice, always made a face and said no. A few years later, he bought his own jewellery store in Edmonton, and he and Sally and Benjy and Benjy's new sister Sharon moved there. It was thousands of kilometres from Toronto, but Sally still kept in close contact with her family, especially her favourite sister, Dora.

Sally's sisters all married. Gert was the first to go — she married Chaim when she was just sixteen and had her first child almost immediately. Pa was furious, but told himself that at least Chaim was Jewish. Sophie was furious, too, because the older girls were supposed to marry first. But she and Dora soon had husbands, too, and eventually so did Molly and Hindl. They all married good Jewish boys that Pa approved of, and they all ended up having children and living quiet lives within a few blocks from each other in Toronto. They remained one another's best friends all through their lives.

But Sally's experience during the war had made her more willing to be with people who weren't "her own kind," and she had many other friends as well. She worked for many years as a stenographer, helping to put her Benjy and Sharon through college and watching in admiration as they developed careers and began to have families of their own. She then enjoyed many years of retirement with Harvey, still happily married to him even though he would always groan whenever she began to sing.

Harvey died in 1999. Sally still lives in her own apartment in Edmonton, where she can sing whenever she wants, but somehow never gets around to it, and where she has frequent visits from Benjy and Sharon, her grandchildren and her great-grandchildren.

During Sally's childhood, her pa received a number of letters from his brother Izzy, the one who had returned to Latvia after deciding he didn't like Canada. Izzy had married, and had two daughters. He wrote about his life as a Cohen in the Jewish community of Riga, which seemed to be doing well even after the USSR took over the country in 1940. But the letters stopped coming soon after the war began and the Germans occupied Latvia in 1941. After the war, Sally and her family did everything they could to try to contact Izzy. But they never heard from him or his wife and children again.

Historical Note

In the early 1930s, Toronto was not the multi-cultural city it has since become. Canada was still a proud member of the British Empire, with much closer ties to Britain than it now has as a member of the Commonwealth. Eighty percent of the population of Toronto was of British origin, and even Jewish Torontonians tended to think of themselves as proud British citizens. As Benny suggested, much of the city — the mayor's office, the police force, and so on — was run by members of the Orange Order, a society for the preservation of Protestant religion and culture that originated in Northern Ireland and that encouraged strong negative feelings about non-British immigrants. There were huge parades in Toronto every year on Orange Day, July 12, with eight to ten thousand marchers and a hundred thousand spectators.

Jews, the largest non-British group in the city, represented just seven percent of the population, and prejudice against them was widespread and socially acceptable. In 1925, an editorial in the most conservative of the large daily newspapers, the *Telegram*, said, "An influx of Jews puts a worm next to the kernel of every fair city where they get hold.

These people have no national tradition. . . . They are not the material out of which to shape a people holding a national spirit."

When World War I started, there were about a hundred thousand Jews in Canada. But from then on, the Canadian government made immigration to Canada difficult for anyone considered "foreign" — especially anyone not white, English-speaking, Christian or with a British background. In his diary, the Canadian Prime Minister Mackenzie King wrote that he wanted "to prevent Jews or other undesirable people from getting in" to Canada, and during the 1920s, it became increasingly unlikely that a Jew from Latvia or any other European country would be allowed into the country. As the 1930s progressed, Canada admitted only a small number of Jewish refugees fleeing from the Nazis — fewer than any other country in the Western world.

But even Jews already living in Canada faced prejudice. Very few Jews were accepted into university programs to become doctors, lawyers or teachers — they were kept out by quotas that limited their numbers; many golf and social clubs accepted no Jewish members; many businesses did not employ Jews. Places of business posted signs saying *No Jews Allowed* or *Gentiles Only,* and the *Zhurnal,* the Yiddish-language newspaper in Toronto, reported a sign at a private beach saying, *No Jews or Dogs Allowed*.

For these reasons as well as for their own comfort, Jews in Toronto did tend to "stick to their own kind." They rarely left their neighbourhood to the west of downtown, around the Kensington market. There, they could find kosher butchers and delis, a variety of synagogues, Jewish social clubs and organizations, many clothing factories owned by and employing Jews, and a lot of other Jews who had come to Canada from all over Europe and spoke many different languages but shared one — Yiddish. There was even a Yiddish theatre, The Standard, at Dundas and Spadina. There were also settlement houses like St. Christopher House, located at the end of Leonard Avenue in a house that had once belonged to the wealthy railway engineer Sir Casimir Gzowski, before the neighbourhood changed character and became a home for Jewish immigrants. The settlement houses were missions of Christian churches with the overall goal of producing converts to Christianity, but St. Chris was also concerned with teaching immigrants Canadian ways and with giving them some useful skills and a social life. Among other activities, it had a playschool, after-school girls' and boys' clubs, sewing classes, athletic teams, a choir, a consulting nurse, well-baby clinics and English classes.

Because of their restricted opportunities, Jews were particularly hard hit by the Great Depression, which started with the crash of the New York stock market on October 24, 1929. A panic led investors to try to sell all their shares, prices fell drastically, and many stocks lost their value in an extremely short time. The stock market crash led to bank failures around the world, falling prices for most goods, massive wage cuts and unemployment. Because so much of its economy depended on exports of raw materials like lumber, Canada was hit hard by the collapse of world trade. The economy fell further than that of any nation other than the United States, and it took longer to recover — not until World War II began in 1939.

Unemployment rose from two percent in 1929 to almost thirty percent in 1932. With so few jobs available, many men began roaming the country, stealing rides in boxcars, constantly moving on because nobody gave them work or welcomed them — including the places they had come from, when they tried to return home. By 1932, there were as many as seventy thousand men riding the rails across Canada. While many people complained about the expense of supporting those less fortunate than themselves, every city and town had soup kitchens, and many charitable organizations and local governments developed "relief" schemes, handing out money, clothing and food after carefully making sure that the recipients were really needy. Many people resented the nosiness of relief inspectors, and felt that accepting relief was a sign of failure. It was only after the bad times had gone on for a few years that the federal government finally took action in 1932 and opened work camps for men who were single, unemployed and homeless.

In the garment industry that employed many Toronto Jews, wages and working conditions had always been poor, and the Depression made things worse. Many workers joined labour unions and various left-wing political parties, including the Communist Party, taking the advice suggested by Karl Marx in his *Communist Manifesto,* commonly stated as: "Workers of the world, unite! You have nothing to lose but your chains." Some of the prejudice against Jews in Toronto came from the belief of many Gentiles that the Jews represented not only a different religion, but also a threat to Canadian society and its entrenched politics and values.

The successful revolution in Russia in 1917 that overthrew the tsar and replaced him with a Communist government not only encouraged those who hoped for similar revolutions in other countries, it also led to the emergence of right-wing groups firmly opposed to power being taken away from those who already had it. Fear of Communism helped bring the Fascists to power in Italy in 1922 and the National Socialist Party, the Nazis, to power in Germany in 1933. Once in power, the Nazis, who believed in racial purity and had a particular distaste for Jews, immediately began to restrict the activities of Jews, boycotting Jewish doctors, lawyers and stores, banning Jews from government jobs and teaching positions, encouraging moves to dismiss Jewish managers and musicians, removing books by Jews from bookstores and libraries, and condoning violence directed against Jews.

The Toronto papers reported all these events in Germany, and knowledge of them encouraged both fear in the Jewish community and approval of the Nazis among various other Canadians. In Quebec, Adrien Arcand, who led a French nationalist movement and called himself the "Canadian führer," considered French-Canadians to be "an honest and upright race which does not want to submit any longer to the exploitation, thievery, perfidy, immorality, filth, corruption, and Bolshevik propaganda of the sons of Judas." Arcand remained a supporter of Nazism throughout his life, and was a mentor to the Holocaust denier Ernst Zündel in the 1960s. While Nazism was less prominent outside of Quebec, it had supporters across Canada.

Nevertheless, the events of 1933 involving the

Swastika Gang, the events at the Beaches, and the riot at Christie Pits were rare — perhaps the only instances of large-scale race-related violence in modern Canada.

Once the heat wave was over, the confrontations stopped. While many Canadians sympathized with the Nazis or simply disliked Jews, their anti-Semitism expressed itself more in attitudes and restrictions — in refusing to accept Jews fleeing from Germany before the war, or survivors of concentration camps after the war, for instance — than in outright violence. Until well after the war, anti-Semitism remained an undercurrent in Canadian life rather than an openly declared policy.

That was obviously not the case in Europe, where the Nazis were responsible for the massacre of millions of Jews and other people they considered undesirable — including, as Sally's family later learned, the murder of twenty-six thousand Jews in Latvia's Rumbula Forest near Riga in 1941. We have to assume that families such as Uncle Izzy's would have been among them.

Most of Toronto's Jewish population lived in the Kensington Market area in the 1930s.

(Above) Originally a mission of the Presbyterian church to
the poor area near the Kensington market, St. Christopher
House offered programs to help neighbourhood families
and immigrants deal with poverty, poor health, illiteracy
and discrimination.
(Below) A homeless man sleeps on a park bench in
Toronto — a common sight during the Depression.

People who couldn't pay their rent could be thrown out onto the street with their meagre possessions.

Many people across Canada had to depend on soup kitchens, such as this one in Montreal.

Many farms in Canada's West failed because of the drought, forcing even more men to seek work elsewhere.

This scene from Annette St. Public School in 1936 is typical of a Toronto schoolyard in the 1930s.

The Book Room at Boys and Girls House, part of the Toronto Public Library. It drew international attention as the first children's library in the British Empire.

People throng the Midway at the Canadian National Exhibition. The Ex continued to draw big crowds even during the Depression.

Some Canadians were very intolerant of Jews. Two signs (top and right) are from Ontario. The photo at the lower left is from Quebec.

The Balmy Beach Canoe Club building. The club had a "Swastika Club" in 1932.

Toronto's *Evening Telegram* page dated August 1, 1932, reports the displaying of swastikas, which triggered the Christie Pits riots.

An image of a baseball game at Christie Pits in 1922, showing the ball diamond and the steep sides leading down to the playing area. The land, formerly a sand quarry, was converted to Willowvale Park after 1910.

The 1931 Harbord Street Junior Champions Baseball Team. A number of the players were also on the 1933 team.

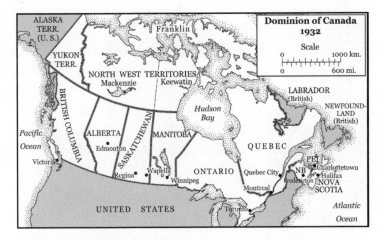

(Above) Canada in 1932–1933.

(Below) The Kensington market neighbourhood, known as the Jewish Market in the thirties. The market was in the area generally bounded by Oxford Street, Baldwin Street, Nassau Street and Spadina Avenue.

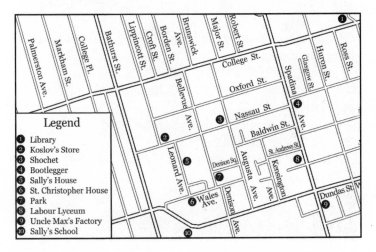

Yiddish Glossary

anti-semit: anti-Semite

bar mitzvah: religious initiation of a Jewish boy of thirteen

bupkis: nothing

cheder: a room or school where Hebrew is taught

chuppah: a canopy under which a Jewish bride and groom make their vows

dreidel: four-sided spinning top

farshtunkener no-goodnik: stinking good-for-nothing

gefilte fish: small cake of chopped fish and other ingredients

gevalt!: cry for help; *"Oy gevalt!"* would mean "God help me!" or "Oh my God!"

gonif: thief

gornisht: nothing

goy: a Gentile; anyone not a Jew; adjective is *goyishe;* plural is *goyim*

Hanukkah: eight-day Jewish holiday that usually falls in December

hechsher: stamp to indicate something is kosher

kayn aynhoreh: "Thank God"; the literal meaning is "no evil eye"

kibitzing: chatting or joking lightheartedly

kosher: Jewish law regarding food

kugel: baked dish, savoury or sweet, of potatoes or noodles

kvetcher: complainer

me shlugt yidn!: They're beating up Jews!

mensch: an admirable or honourable person

meshugge/meshuggeneh: crazy

oy: exclamation of alarm

Passover: the Jewish spring festival marking the
Israelites being freed from slavery in Egypt

Pesach: the Passover festival

Rosh Hashanah: festival celebrating the Jewish new
year

schmaltz: melted chicken fat

seder: Jewish service/dinner at the beginning of
Passover

Shabbes: Jewish sabbath

sha shtil: shut up

shaygetz: a negative term for a non-Jewish boy

shochet: person authorized by a rabbi to slaughter
animals in a kosher fashion

shul: synagogue

sitting *shiva:* gathering together in someone's house
and mourning together

shmendrick: someone of no account

synagogue: the building where Jews assemble for
religions observance or instruction

trayf: any food which is non-kosher

trombenik: braggart; a loudmouthed troublemaker

Yid: if pronounced "Yeed," a Jew; mispronounced
Yid" (like "kid"), an offensive term for a Jewish
person; adjective is *Yiddishe*

Yom Kippur: the Day of Atonement, following the
Jewish new year; the most solemn day of the year

zayde: grandfather

Acknowledgments

Grateful acknowledgment is made for permission to reprint the following:

Cover portrait: (colourized) courtesy of Joyce Zweig.
Cover background: Detail (tinted) from People eating at a soup kitchen, Library and Archives Canada/PA-168131.

Page 196: Jewish Market Day, Kensington Market, Toronto, Ont., 1924, Metro Toronto Reference Library, T11552.
Page 197 upper: St. Christopher House, Toronto, Archives of Ontario, F 1075-13, H 1363, M.O. Hammond Fonds.
Page 197 lower: Unemployed man sleeping on park bench, City of Toronto Archives, Fonds 1257, Series 1057, Item 4636.
Page 198: Eviction from a slum, City of Toronto Archives, Fonds 1244, Item 8030.
Page 199: People eating at a soup kitchen, Library and Archives Canada/PA-168131.
Page 200 upper: Threshing machine during Depression years, Glenbow Museum, 2291-2.
Page 200 lower: Transient man riding the rails, Glenbow Museum, NC-54-3604.
Page 201: Cluster of schoolgirls, skipping, 1936, City of Toronto Archives, *Globe and Mail* Collection, Fonds 1266, Item 39567.
Page 202: Room at Boys and Girls House, Toronto Public Library, photo from City of Toronto Archives, SCN268-1998N.
Page 203: Crowd scene on Midway, September 1, 1925, City of Toronto Archives, *Globe and Mail* Collection, Fonds 1266, Item 6127.
Page 204 upper: *Gentiles Only* sign, found at a resort northeast of Toronto, ca. 1935, Ontario Jewish Archives, photo 6161.
Page 204 right: *No Jews Wanted* sign at Jackson's Point, ON, 1938 (detail), Ontario Jewish Archives, photo 1181.
Page 204 left: Canadian Jewish Congress.
Page 205: Balmy Beach Club, Toronto Public Library, Repro # 974-11-2.
Page 206: The *Evening Telegram*, August 1, 1932 (detail), Sun Media Corp.

Page 207: Willowvale Park – Baseball, May 13, 1922, City of Toronto Archives, Series 372, Sub Series 52, Item 1011.
Page 208: Harbord Street Collegiate Junior Champions, September 6, 1931, City of Toronto Archives, DPW52-1492.

Page 209: Maps by Paul Heersink/Paperglyphs. Map data © 2002 Government of Canada with permission from Natural Resources Canada.

The publisher would like to thank Dr. Irving Abella, co-author of *None Is Too Many*, and Dr. Bill Waiser, author of *All Hell Can't Stop Us: The On-to-Ottawa Trek and Regina Riot*, for vetting the manuscript. Thanks also to Barbara Hehner for fact-checking the manuscript.

About the Author

Perry Nodelman's character, Sally Cohen, lived in a time and place very much like that of his mother and father when they were young. "And so," he says, "I hit on the brilliant idea of interviewing my parents about their childhoods and what they remembered of what it was like to be young and Jewish in Toronto in the early 1930s. Neither of them had been at Christie Pits during the riot. But both had been Jewish in what was a surprisingly intolerant city in the early thirties, and both knew what it was like to be poor in the Depression."

Perry's father, he recalls, "was always a great storyteller. He talked of things like the white tuxedo his mother bought him and the band that resulted from it, with much drama and great gusto. As a teller of stories about himself, my father had what I think of as a hyperbole complex — if he'd once swum across a pond and came second in a race, he'd tell us about how he swam across Lake Ontario using just one hand and was given a gigantic trophy by the Prime Minister, who told him he was the best thing since sliced bread. But there was always a little truth at the heart of his stories. Many details of Benny's life came from my father's stories of his childhood. It saddens me that he died this past April, and never got to learn about Benny."

Sally herself very much springs from Perry's mother's stories. "She, too, was one of six girls. Her mother and father had emigrated from Latvia in the early years of the twentieth century. Her family lived a few blocks from the Kensington Market and her father had a truck and bought vegetables from farmers to be sold in the Toronto markets. . . . My mother was able to give detailed answers to my questions about things like what her family typically ate for supper and how the *shochet* killed a chicken and what happened on a normal day in school."

After Perry's mother read the first draft of his story, it took her some time before she could bring herself to talk to him about it. "I imagined it was because she was mad that I'd misused her memories and told a different story about someone else. But when she finally did talk, it turned out she had been deeply affected by the story and the intense memories it evoked. It brought many things back to her — not all of them pleasant."

As the story and the Historical Note describe, Toronto in the 1930s was not racially tolerant. "Both my parents told me that there had been a sign that said *No Jews or Dogs Allowed* at a private beach somewhere near Toronto," Perry says. "But while the Toronto Jewish newspaper the *Yiddisher Zhurnal* did report such a sign at the time, and while other people who spoke of these years in later life also had firm memories of it, there's no actual archival evidence that the sign existed. It might have just been a rumour that floated through the Jewish community — but if so, it was an only slightly exaggerated version of the many actual *No Jews* or *Gentiles Only* signs that we know for a fact were common."

Perry's father obviously passed on his love of story. "I like reading, thinking, making things up," Perry says. "As a child, my favourite game was making papier-mâché puppets and cardboard-box stages and putting on shows for my brothers."

Perry is professor emeritus of children's literature at the University of Winnipeg, and he continues to indulge his love of reading as the editor of *Canadian Children's Literature/Littérature canadienne pour la jeunesse.* He is the author of *The Same Place but Different, A Completely Different Place* and *Behaving Bradley,* and co-author, with Carol Matas, of the "Minds" series beginning with the book *Of Two Minds.* His books about children's literature include *Words About Pictures: The Narrative Art of Children's Picture Books* and, with colleague Mavis Reimer, *The Pleasures of Children's Literature,* a textbook used in universities across North America and elsewhere.

◇

While the characters and events of *Not a Nickel to Spare* are fictional, I based many of the details and incidents on my parents' memories of their life in Toronto in the thirties. I am grateful to Lonnie Nodelman, who died in 2006, and to Dorothy Berkan Nodelman, for their willingness to share their fascinating stories and for so many other things.

While I consulted a number of books and articles, my knowledge of the events at the Beaches and Christie Pits in 1933 comes mainly from two sources: Cyril H. Levitt and William Shaffir's *The Riot at Christie Pits* and the 1932–1933 issues of the *Toronto Daily Star*. The ready availability of the *Star* archive on the internet (http://thestar.pagesofthepast.ca/) made my task much easier and much more interesting. Browsing in it, I even found my own birth notice.

I learned much about the effects of the Depression from Pierre Berton's *The Great Depression, 1929–1939* and Barry Broadfoot's *Ten Lost Years*. Some of the more thrilling events in the life of Benny Applebaum are based on ones the boxer Sammy Luftspring reports in his autobiography, *Call Me Sammy*.

My thanks to Bob Desroches for visiting the market and the Pits and bringing back visual evidence, to Carol Matas and Sandy Bogart Johnston for careful reading and good advice, and to my family — Billie Nodelman, Josh and Jenny Nodelman, Asa Nodelman and Jeanne Hudek, and Alice Nodelman and Zach Brown — for listening to me go on and on about the riot and not threatening their own uprising.

— *P.N.*

While the events described and some of the characters in this book may be based on actual historical events and real people, Sally Cohen is a fictional character created by the author, and her diary is a work of fiction.

Library and Archives Canada Cataloguing in Publication

Nodelman, Perry
    Not a nickel to spare : the Great Depression diary of Sally Cohen, Toronto, 1932 / Perry Nodelman.

(Dear Canada)
ISBN 978-0-439-96130-1

1. Depressions--1929--Ontario--Toronto--Juvenile fiction.
2. Jews--Ontario--Toronto--Juvenile fiction. 3. Antisemitism--Ontario--Toronto--Juvenile fiction. 4. Toronto (Ont.)-- History--Juvenile fiction. I. Title. II. Series.

PS8577.O33N68 2007   jC813'.54   C2006-906552-7

6 5 4 3 2 1   Printed in Canada   07 08 09 10 11

The display type was set in Luna ITC Bold.
The text was set in Galliard.
First printing May 2007

Alone in an Untamed Land, The Filles du Roi *Diary of Hélène St. Onge* by Maxine Trottier

Banished from Our Home, The Acadian Diary of Angélique Richard by Sharon Stewart

Brothers Far from Home, The World War I Diary of Eliza Bates by Jean Little

The Death of My Country, The Plains of Abraham Diary of Geneviève Aubuchon by Maxine Trottier

Footsteps in the Snow, The Red River Diary of Isobel Scott by Carol Matas

If I Die Before I Wake, The Flu Epidemic Diary of Fiona Macgregor by Jean Little

No Safe Harbour, The Halifax Explosion Diary of Charlotte Blackburn by Julie Lawson

An Ocean Apart, The Gold Mountain Diary of Chin Mei-ling by Gillian Chan

Orphan at My Door, The Home Child Diary of Victoria Cope by Jean Little

A Prairie as Wide as the Sea, The Immigrant Diary of Ivy Weatherall by Sarah Ellis

A Ribbon of Shining Steel, The Railway Diary of Kate Cameron by Julie Lawson

A Rebel's Daughter, The 1837 Rebellion Diary of Arabella Stevenson by Janet Lunn

A Season for Miracles, Twelve Tales of Christmas

A Trail of Broken Dreams, The Gold Rush Diary of Harriet Palmer by Barbara Haworth-Attard

Turned Away, The World War II Diary of Devorah Bernstein by Carol Matas

Whispers of War, The War of 1812 Diary of Susanna Merritt by Kit Pearson

Winter of Peril, The Newfoundland Diary of Sophie Loveridge by Jan Andrews

With Nothing But Our Courage, The Loyalist Diary of Mary MacDonald by Karleen Bradford

Go to www.scholastic.ca/dearcanada for information on the Dear Canada Series — see inside the books, read an excerpt or a review, post a review, and more.